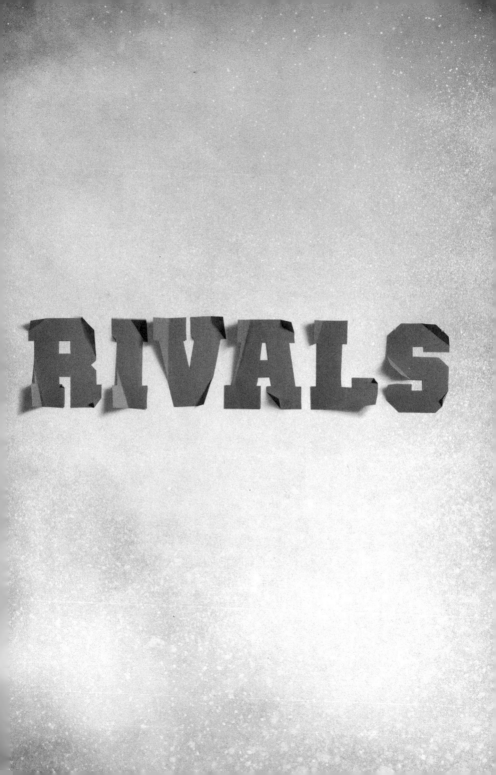

RIVALS

TOMMY GREENWALD

AMULET BOOKS

NEW YORK

For all those dedicated parents, teachers, and coaches
who do it the right way

Cataloging-in-Publication Data has been applied for and may be obtained from the Library of Congress.

ISBN 978-1-4197-4827-1

Text © 2021 Tommy Greenwald
Book design by Heather Kelly

Printed and bound in U.S.A.
10 9 8 7 6 5 4 3 2 1

Amulet Books are available at special discounts when purchased in quantity for premiums and promotions as well as fundraising or educational use. Special editions can also be created to specification. For details, contact specialsales@abramsbooks.com or the address below.

Amulet Books® is a registered trademark of Harry N. Abrams, Inc.

ABRAMS The Art of Books
195 Broadway, New York, NY 10007
abramsbooks.com

*We do not stop playing because we grow old,
we grow old because we stop playing.*
—Benjamin Franklin and George Bernard Shaw, among others

You know what's weird?

When you're falling through the air, about to crash into a hard wooden floor and get really badly hurt or possibly die, you have a lot of time to think.

Which is good, because I have a ton of stuff to think about as I fall.

The first thing I think is, this isn't as scary as I thought. I mean, it's definitely scary, but it's also calm.

And silent.

Like, the world stops.

I keep falling, and I keep thinking.

I think about everything that led up to this moment.

I think about my mom and dad.

I think about not wanting to die.

I think about how much it's going to hurt when I land, if I don't die.

I think about what kind of injuries I'm going to have and how long it will take for me to get better.

I think about how the injuries might be so bad, I won't be able to play basketball again for a long time. Or ever. Or maybe I'll be able to play, but I won't be as good as I am right now.

And I think about how that might not be the worst thing in the world.

I hit the floor.

I hear a SLAM! *Then a* CRACK!

And everything goes dark.

FIRST HALF
Four Months Earlier

PROWLING WITH THE PANTHERS
A MIDDLE SCHOOL SPORTS BLOG BY ALFIE JENKS
MONDAY, NOVEMBER 5

Hoops Season Kicks Off with Middle School Tradition

You can feel the crispness in the air. You can try to ignore the holiday commercials popping up on television, but you can hear the rustle of winter coats being removed from mothballed closets all over town.

That can only mean one thing: It's basketball season in Walthorne!

This is a town that takes its basketball extremely seriously; four Walthorne hometown heroes have made it to the NBA over the years and one to the WNBA, while many student-athletes have received Division I scholarships. Girls and boys all over town are getting ready for the season at every level, from the district champ Walthorne Wildcats high school team right down to the kindergarten Superkitten League.

One tradition that everyone looks forward to is the season-opening game between the Walthorne North Middle School Cougars and the Walthorne South Middle School Panthers. Since 1986, these two rivals have played each other twice a year: the first game of the season and the last game of the season. And it's always an exciting, fun-filled event.

I caught up with key members of each team as they were practicing for the big game. Austin Chambers, fourteen, is the captain of the Walthorne North squad. A point guard, Austin is the son of Frank Chambers, local legend and former star shooting guard at Penn State. "This is going to be our year," Austin told us. "We've got a strong team and a great bunch of guys. Keep an eye out for Clay Elkind, our center. He's turning into a huge weapon for us." Across town, fourteen-year-old Carter Haswell, a young phenom who already stands six feet, two inches tall and was all-state last year as a seventh grader, captains the Walthorne South squad. "I think we could go far," said Carter. "I like our chances a lot, and Benny Walters is the best coach in the league. But Walthorne North is always tough, and they'll be a great first challenge for us."

These two young men will lead their teams onto the floor this Friday at Walthorne South gym. Game time is 4 pm. (And just a personal note: I will be broadcasting the game LIVE on our middle school radio station and website! So feel free to tune in.)

WWMS
WALTHORNE SOUTH RADIO

ALFIE: Testing, testing 123 . . .
            Is this thing on?

CARTER: If you're talking to me, I can't
            hear you.

ALFIE: Dang it! This equipment is pretty old.
            Mr. Rashad said he was trying to get
            us some new stuff but he uh . . . so,
            yeah, sorry, hold on a sec . . . how
            about now?

CARTER: Oh sweet, now I got you. Yup,
            we're good.

ALFIE: Cool. (BANGS THE MIC)
            Okay, so, yeah! Welcome to Talking
            Sports on WWMS. It's Wednesday,
            November 7th, and my name is
            Alfie Jenks, sports editor and
            head sportswriter.

CARTER: So, will anyone actually, like,
            hear this?

ALFIE: What do you mean?

CARTER: Like, does anyone listen to your show?

ALFIE: Oh absolutely.

CARTER: Like who?

ALFIE: I mean, well, you know, it's mostly just for fun and stuff, but like, I think my mom definitely listens.

CARTER: (LAUGHS) HA! Cool. Well in that case, I'll try not to swear.

ALFIE: Thank you.

CARTER: What kind of name is Alfie for a girl, anyway?

ALFIE: I'm named after my grandfather. I like it. Why, you don't like it?

CARTER: Uh, no, it's cool.

ALFIE: I think so, too. So, anyway, yeah, once again welcome to the show everybody. That voice you hear belongs to Carter Haswell, eighth grade basketball star and captain of the Walthorne South Middle School Panthers. We're here to talk about the upcoming game, the first game of the season against your archrivals, the Walthorne North Cougars. Carter, what are your thoughts?

CARTER: Uh, my thoughts?

ALFIE: Yeah. You know, like, your thoughts about the game and stuff.

CARTER: My thoughts. Got it. Well, my thoughts are that I hope we win.

ALFIE: Cool.

CARTER: Cool.

ALFIE: Everyone's been looking forward to this game since the end of last year, when the two teams battled it out for the league championship and you guys beat them in the finals by three.

CARTER: That was pretty awesome, especially winning in that fancy new gym they built.

ALFIE: Yeah. I wonder when we're gonna get a
              gym like that.

CARTER: Probably never.

ALFIE: So now it's a new season, though, and
              Walthorne North has a lot of tall
              players, especially their center, Clay
              Elkind. What's the plan to contain
              them? Are you gonna play zone, maybe
              a box and one, or do you think you
              can handle them playing man-to-
              man? Are you concerned about their
              pick-and-roll?

CARTER: Whoa. You know a lot about basketball.
              Like, more than me even.

ALFIE: I love basketball.

CARTER: Cool. I like basketball, too.

ALFIE: Do you love it?

CARTER: Uh, sure, I guess. I'm not, like,
              obsessed with it or anything.

ALFIE: That's so weird because people are
              saying you're, like, one of the

best players to ever come out of
Walthorne, and you're not even in
high school yet.

CARTER: I don't pay attention to any of that
            stuff. A lot of people take basketball
            too seriously if you ask me. I mean,
            it's just a game, right?

ALFIE: If you say so. So if you don't take it
            seriously, how did you get so good? Do
            you practice a lot?

CARTER: I practice when I feel like practicing,
            which is a lot, but, like it's not all
            I ever do. Do you play an instrument?

ALFIE: No.

CARTER: Oh. Well, I love playing guitar, but
            I'm way worse at that than I am at
            basketball. It's like, some things
            you're really good at, and some things
            you're not, and that's just the way it
            is, you know? With basketball, people
            tell me I have a feel for the game. I
            guess that's part of it.

ALFIE: Plus you're tall and super athletic.

CARTER: Yeah well, that's all luck.

ALFIE: I guess so. Well, it's almost time for
            next class, so thanks for coming on
            the show.

CARTER: No problem.

ALFIE: Oh wait! I almost forgot, the school
            asked me to announce that the town is
            doing this online pep rally thing, and
            they want us to encourage people to
            go on there and say supportive things
            about all our sports teams and show
            some school spirit!

CARTER: Oh yeah, I heard about that. I
            guess that sounds fun, so yeah, for
            whoever's listening out there, check
            it out—wait, what's it called again?

ALFIE: Walthornespirit.com

CARTER: Right yeah, Walthornespirit.com. I
            guess, like, lots of kids are going
            to be on there getting psyched up
            for the winter sports season, so
            all the boys and girls teams are

counting on everyone for support and stuff. Thanks.

ALFIE: Thank <u>you</u>, Carter! This has been Alfie Jenks, Talking Sports. Be sure to tune in next week, when my guest will be seventh grade gymnastics star Rebecca Smythe.

SO YOU GOING ON THIS ONLINE THING NOW?

CAN'T RIGHT NOW I GOT MY TRAINING IN A FEW MINUTES, WILL CHECK IT OUT WHEN I GET HOME

THAT PRIVATE COACH DUDE? YOU'RE STILL DOING THAT?

YEAH
HE'S AN AMAZING COACH,
YOU SHOULD THINK ABOUT TRAINING WITH HIM TOO
ALTHO YOU'RE ALREADY WAY BETTER THAN ME AT THIS POINT LOL

HA I DON'T KNOW ABOUT THAT BUT THX

ANYWAY I GTG BUT DON'T FORGET TO GO ONLINE TO THAT THING,
COACH WILL BE MAD IF WE DON'T,
I TOLD EVERYONE ELSE THEY GOTTA DO IT TOO

OKAY MAYBE I'LL CHECK IT OUT

WALTHORNESPIRIT.COM

WELCOME TO WALTHORNESPIRIT.COM, AN ONLINE PEP RALLY TO GET THE WHOLE TOWN EXCITED ABOUT THE WINTER SPORTS SEASON! PLEASE BE SURE TO POST SUPPORTIVE THINGS ABOUT YOUR FRIENDS AND TEAMMATES FOR ALL SPORTS! *PLEASE NOTE* THIS SITE WILL BE MONITORED AND NEGATIVE COMMENTS WILL NOT BE TOLERATED!

Wednesday at 6:20 pm

Carter Yo everyone did you guys check out my radio interview with Alfie today? #rockstar
She was asking me about the little test we got with Walthorne North this Friday to open the season, who's comin and who's down with getting LOUD?!?!

Like · Reply

Wednesday at 6:22 pm

Janeece I'll be there
And the first girls game is next Monday and hope to see y'all there too

Like · Reply

Wednesday at 6:25 pm

Abner I'll be there Carter to see you whup up on those North boys

Like · Reply

Wednesday at 6:26 pm

Briscoe I'll see if I can clear my sked

Like · Reply

Wednesday at 6:28 pm

Lucas Every1 wear red and if you sit behind the hoops you are hereby ordered to go nuts during every foul shot taken by North

Like · Reply

Wednesday at 6:30 pm

Carter U know it

Like · Reply

Wednesday at 6:33 pm

Clementine i will say those boys do look cute in those little uniforms with the shorty shorts

Like · Reply

Wednesday at 6:34 pm

Briscoe C'mon Clem throw some love to the football players

Like · Reply

Wednesday at 6:36 pm

Sham Back off son, it's basketball season. Please continue my dear

Like · Reply

Wednesday at 6:38 pm

Clementine Nah I'm done

Like · Reply

Wednesday at 6:41 pm

Sadie Sorry Briscoe, Clem's right
Basketball players are cuter because they're not all covered up
You can see Amir's gorgeous face
And Carter's got that pretty blond hair flowing as he runs up and
down the court

Like · Reply

Wednesday at 6:43 pm

Janeece Whoa Sadie settle down

Like · Reply

Wednesday at 6:44 pm

Carter No don't, keep going ☺

Like · Reply

Wednesday at 6:46 pm

Eddy Yo what about me? Am I pretty too?

Like · Reply

Wednesday at 6:47 pm

North4Eva You guys are so cute and funny hahahaha lolol but meanwhile over at W-North we're practicing RIGHT NOW with one thing in mind, TAKE DOWN W-SOUTH and that's exactly what's gonna happen
so u all keep passing notes back and forth like fifth graders, we'll pass the rock, and we'll see who comes out on top Friday

Like · Reply

Wednesday at 6:50 pm

Amir Who is this dude
You up past your bedtime?

Like · Reply

Wednesday at 6:52 pm

North4Eva Doesn't matter who I am it only matters what I do on the floor, who's with me?

Like · Reply

Wednesday at 6:53 pm

Chase Can I be part of this fun little pep rally even though I go to Walthorne Academy? I play hockey which is much harder than basketball btw. Hey South how's your hockey team, oh that's right you don't have a hockey team
But I think I saw some of your parents cleaning up the rink after our last game

Like · Reply

Wednesday at 6:54 pm

Kevin Chase man, they're gonna kick you off of here

Like · Reply

Wednesday at 6:56 pm

Lucas What kind of a lame name is Chase

Like · Reply

Wednesday at 6:57 pm

Sham I know right??

Like · Reply

Wednesday at 7:00 pm

North4Eva The kind of name that smells like money
As opposed to Sham which, uh, doesn't

Like · Reply

Wednesday at 7:01 pm

Chase Thank you my friend

Like · Reply

Wednesday at 7:02 pm

North4Eva No hard feelings tho right fellas?

Like · Reply

Wednesday at 7:03 pm

Admin Please be advised that this board is being monitored for inappropriate content, and appropriate action will be taken when deemed necessary.

Like · Reply

Wednesday at 7:04 pm

Carter Yo can everyone chill please

Like · Reply

Wednesday at 7:06 pm

Austin Whoa just reading this stuff now, not cool seriously

Like · Reply

Wednesday at 7:09 pm

Chase Hahahaha what are you guys, the principals? Do you want to see us in your office?

Like · Reply

Wednesday at 7:11 pm

Clay This is nuts

Like · Reply

Wednesday at 7:12 pm

North4eva I know right?

Like · Reply

Wednesday at 7:13 pm

Clay Austin dude
You better hope Coach doesn't see this

Like · Reply

Wednesday at 7:16 pm

Ashley Hope to see everyone at Walthorne North girls volleyball next Tuesday against Caldwell Middle!

Like · Reply

Wednesday at 7:18 pm

Lucas Ooh Ashley I can't wait, don't forget to get a mani pedi and blowdry your hair and maybe get a nose job before the big game! #northgirlsareplastic

Like · Reply

Wednesday at 7:19 pm

Janeece Lucas shut it, not funny

Like · Reply

Wednesday at 7:23 pm

Admin Please be advised that certain comments are being deleted and certain accounts are in danger of being blocked from this site.

Like · Reply

Wednesday at 7:25 pm

Clay Lol I don't think this is going well so far you guys

Like · Reply

CARTER

I slam my computer shut.

The whole online thing was supposed to be chill, just talking about how we're going to win and where we're going to hang out after, stuff like that. And yeah, maybe a little flirting. But instead, everyone tries to act like high school kids.

The thing is, no one should be surprised. I mean, what did they think was going to happen? Walthorne North is our rival. More than our rival, actually. We hate them. I know I shouldn't use that word. We dislike them a lot, okay? They're across town, but they might as well be across the universe. That's how different they are.

I mean, I don't know any of those kids personally, but I know what they are. They think they're special. When they turn sixteen, their parents give them cars, and when they turn eighteen, their parents give them new cars.

That's what I've heard, anyway.

So yeah, I don't like them, but I'll give them one thing: They know how to play basketball.

Last year, we played them twice and went to a few other

games to scout them. The first time we walked into their gym, my friend Eddy, who's Black, looked a little nervous, and when I asked him why, he said, "Look around, man. This school is whiter than your left butt cheek." And he wasn't wrong. At South, we have all kinds of kids. At North, they have all kinds of rich white kids, and not too many of anyone else.

Maybe that's why they have such a cocky attitude. They think they're different from us, and they are. But they also think they're better than us, and they aren't.

And it can get a little intimidating over there, I'm not gonna lie. But there was this one time when Coach Benny came with us, and he told us to just keep on walking and hold our heads up high. A bunch of people came over to shake Coach Benny's hand, because he's pretty famous, like a legend basically. He used to coach Walthorne High for, like, thirty years and he turned them into a powerhouse, but then he got older and didn't want all the pressure, so he came down to Walthorne South Middle. But he's still the GOAT. And when we went to watch North play and Coach was with us, it felt different.

He protected us.

My parents don't let me go on social media very much. They're always telling me that studies have proven it does way more harm than good. After seeing this stuff go back and forth in this ridiculous online pep rally thing, I think maybe they're right.

A few minutes after I log off, I get a text from Clay.

> PJ THAT WAS NUTS DUDE! BTW WHO WAS NORTH4EVA, DO YOU KNOW? CHASE TEXTED ME HE WAS GONNA HAVE SOME FUN BUT I DIDN'T REALIZE HE'D GO THAT FAR. WHOA

Chase Crawford doesn't even go to our school. He goes to Walthorne Academy, but he's friends with a lot of kids on the team. He also has an indoor basketball court, which is pretty sweet. As for PJ, that's my nickname. It's a dumb nickname, but there's a story behind it. My dad travels a lot for his job, but he always makes it home for my games. I think if he missed one, he might literally jump off a bridge or something. Anyway, there was this one time he was halfway across the country and his flight was delayed and I had a big game, so he hired a private jet and made it back for the second half. I was really psyched that he made it, but ever since then, my friends and teammates have called me PJ—for private jet.

I actually don't mind it as a nickname, even though I think they're kind of making fun of me and my family and my dad for being the kind of guy who would rent a plane, but whatever.

I decide not to text Clay back. Then, ten minutes later, I change my mind.

ICE THE LEG. LAST PRACTICE TOMORROW BEFORE THE GAME.

WWMS
WALTHORNE SOUTH RADIO

ALFIE: Hello everyone, my name is Alfie Jenks,
                sports reporter for WWMS News. Welcome
                to the very exciting first game of the
                year between Walthorne South Middle
                School and Walthorne North Middle
                School! We're just about ready to get
                underway, with South's Amir Watkins
                getting set to tip against North's
                Clay Elkind . . .

                . . . Just underway in the second
                quarter, with North leading 14–10, and
                Carter Haswell takes the ball upcourt.
                Carter is for sure the best player on
                floor, the captain of the South team,
                but he is off to a somewhat slow
                start tonight, with only four points
                on 2-for-6 shooting. Ooh, but there
                he goes, puts a spin move on North
                defender Austin Chambers that leaves
                Chambers stumbling! Carter passes to
                Eddy Dixon on the wing, Eddy dumps
                the ball into Lucas Burdeen, Lucas is
                defended well by North Center Clay
                Elkind, who is the tallest player
                on either team. Lucas sends the ball

back out to Carter at the top of
the key, Carter takes two dribbles
between his legs, then launches a
three-pointer . . . perfect form as
usual . . . It's good, nothing but
net! The crowd roars! Carter Haswell
now has seven points as South closes
to 14–13 . . .

. . . South calls timeout. With 4:15
left to play in the third quarter,
South leads 36–34. This game has more
than lived up to the hype! So far,
if you ask me, the story of the game
has been two performances. Carter
Haswell is playing his usual amazing
game; after a quiet first quarter, he
has started to pour it on, and by
my calculations he has exactly half
of South's points, with 18 points,
3 assists, and 7 rebounds. But I would
have to say that the surprise of the
game is North center Clay Elkind,
who has used his size and skill to
lead his team with 13 points and
8 rebounds, even though he appears to
be limping slightly. North captain
Austin Chambers is right behind him
with 9 points and is doing a nice job

handling the pressure at point guard. There's the horn, the players are coming back onto the court . . .

. . . Well basketball fans, it all comes down to this: just twenty-two seconds left in this game, and North is leading 52–51. South Coach Benny Walters just used his last time-out to draw up a play, and no doubt the ball is going to superstar Carter Haswell, who has been a one-man wrecking crew out there. Eddy Dixon inbounds the ball to Carter, who takes it across the half-court line . . . he's being guarded by Austin Chambers, who is not as quick as Carter but is a very tough player . . . Kevin Booker comes over from the wing to double-team Carter, they are determined not to let him get a shot off . . . Oh, Carter slips between them and now he's got a clear lane to the basket! Carter takes one last dribble . . . goes up for the layup . . . and oh my goodness what a block by Clay Elkind! Clay comes out of nowhere and leaps way up into the air to swat the shot away! The clock expires and North wins! North wins by one point! It must be sweet revenge after such a painful loss in the finals last year! But wait a minute . . . Clay is down. Clay is down on the court, grabbing his knee and crying out in pain. The North team is celebrating, but one of their players, their star player, is down. Now they see him. A few of the coaches help him up. Oh, it looks like he can't put any pressure on his left leg. Clay Elkind looks badly hurt. What a terrible way to end a magnificent game. Clay was the MVP out there for his team, but now it looks like it could come at a terrible price! Stand by, I will try to get more information for you, as North wins this opening game thriller!

It's incredible how fast you can go from being happy to being not happy.

When I see Clay block that kid Carter's shot, I start to freak out celebrating. I mean, I'm jumping all over the place, yelling in my teammates' faces, just totally going nuts. We won! We got revenge and beat South!

And then somebody says, "Clay's not getting up."

I run over and see Clay on the ground, thrashing around, like one of those bluefish on the deck of my dad's boat. His mouth is open like he wants to scream, but no sound is coming out.

"Clay!" I say. "Buddy! You okay, man?"

He looks at me but doesn't say anything. He blinks a few times, and I see a tear falling down his cheek.

I look away.

Adults start rushing onto the court.

As I step back, I hear Clay say his first words since getting hurt.

"This is your fault!" he screams, but I'm not sure who he's talking to.

"Dang, nasty block, dude," I say to the kid as he's lying on the ground. I quickly realize he's hurt, though, so I give him a pat on the shoulder, then go back to our bench.

I grab some water as teammates and coaches give me high fives, pats on the back, stuff like that. I played decent, not great, there were things I could have done better, but no biggie. I'm going to hear all about it from Coach Benny, anyway.

I scan the crowd for my mom and find her, talking to my friend Eddy's mom. She sees me and waves. I wave back, then feel a yank on my arm. It's Alfie, the sports reporter girl.

"Great game!" she says. "You played so great!"

"I played okay, but thanks."

She sticks a microphone in my face. "Can you tell the listeners what happened on that last play?"

"Uh, well, I thought I had them beat, split the double-team, but then this kid came out of nowhere and swatted it away. It was a great play."

"And now it looks like he's hurt," Alfie says. We both watch as some adults help the injured kid walk to the bench, where he sits down so they can keep working on him. Alfie turns back to me. "I noticed he was limping a bit throughout the game, did you see that, too?"

I nod. "Yeah, I think I know what you mean, but you know, he wasn't playing like he was hurt, that's for sure. He played amazing."

My mom has worked her way down to the court and heads straight over to me. "I'm so proud of you, honey!"

"Thanks, Ma, but we lost."

"I don't care. Just seeing you out there, playing so well. I enjoy it so much."

"Cool."

I love that watching me play makes her happy.

I don't love that it's one of the only things that makes her happy.

She kisses my sweaty forehead. "I gotta get back to work. Be home late." My mom works at an assisted living facility. They let her out of work so she can go to the games, but otherwise she's there almost all the time.

"Your mom seems awesome," Alfie says, as my mom walks away. "She must be so proud of you."

I nod. "She is."

"Is your dad here, too?"

I hesitate for a second.

"Was there something else you wanted to ask me about the game?"

My dad and I head to Currier's Steakhouse. It's just me and him, which is the way it's been after every game I've played since fifth grade. We eat steak at Currier's, and he tells me the few things I did right and the many things I did wrong.

"Pretty exciting game," he says, as he backs his giant Range Rover into a parking spot. "You feel good?"

"Yeah, I guess so."

"Well, you guys won, and that's the main thing."

The truth is, winning's not the main thing, at least as far as my dad is concerned. The main thing is that I play well. The other main thing is that I'm the best player on the team. But in this game, neither of those things was exactly true, so he's not in a great mood.

My dad stares at his phone until the salads come, when he sighs and looks up at me. "Obviously you looked a little rusty out there. Your shot wasn't falling, your ball distribution was shaky, and you need to get in a lot better shape. But you had active hands on D, so that's good."

"I thought I played okay. Anyway, it was great to see Clay pick up the slack."

As soon as I say that, I wish I hadn't.

"I'll tell you something," my dad says. "Clay could really become something special. Tough break on the injury, though. You know anything about how long he'll be out?"

"I heard the coach talking to his parents, and it sounds like they think it might be serious."

"Oh, man. He could be out for a while." My dad winks at me. "But the good news is, you'll see more of the ball."

The steaks come, and we dig in. My dad isn't finished talking about Clay. "I hadn't seen him in a few months, he's like a different person. When did he get so tall? Wasn't he basically your height last year?"

"Yeah, just about."

"Crazy. I mean, you were taller than him for years. Remember?"

I don't answer, because I don't need to. Of course I remember. My height is one of my family's favorite and least-favorite topics.

My dad is six-four and played basketball at Penn State. My mom is five-nine and was all-state in high school. So of course everyone thought I would end up becoming a really tall, really excellent basketball player—especially my parents. And everything went according to plan at first. I loved basketball, I was good at it, and I was tall. In fact, I was the tallest kid in my grade, until around fourth grade. Then the other kids started to catch up with me. Then the other kids started to pass me. Then my fifth grade coach moved me from center to power forward. Then my sixth grade coach moved me from power forward to small forward. And last year, I started playing guard.

As much as I loved the game, I wasn't sure it loved me back.

Earlier this year, my mom took me to the doctor for a check-up. She said she was curious about my height and asked the doctor how tall he thought I was going to get.

"To be honest," the doctor said, "I'm not sure Austin is going to get much taller at all. In fact, he may be done growing."

My mom smiled and said, "Well, that is surprising! Thank you so much."

As we walked out of the doctor's office, she said, "We're never going back there again."

So yeah, I'm well aware that I used to be taller than Clay.

While my dad and I are eating our steaks, a woman comes over and lingers behind our table. We're used to this. My dad is kind of a local celebrity because of his basketball career.

"I'm so sorry to bother you, but are you Frank Chambers?"

My dad gives her a friendly nod. "I am indeed. What's your name?"

"Oh, hi, I'm Rebecca. It's so nice to meet you. My parents used to watch your games on TV all the time."

"That's great to hear, tell them hi for me."

"Oh, I will!" The woman blushes and smiles shyly, and I think she might be flirting with my dad. Then she looks over at me. "Are you Frank's son? You must be, you look just like him, with that jet-black hair and those gorgeous blue eyes."

Yup, that clinches it—she's flirting with him, all right.

"My name's Austin," I say, silently predicting her next question.

"Are you a basketball star like your dad?"

Nailed it.

"Not quite," I tell her.

"He'll get there," my dad says.

She gives me a pat on the shoulder. "Well, I'm sure we'll be watching you on TV before too long."

We all chat for another minute or so, she asks for a picture, and my dad stays friendly the whole time, even at the end, when she asks him, "Did you end up becoming a professional player?" and he has to tell her, "No."

When it's time for dessert, my dad announces loudly: "A sweet win calls for a sweet treat!" It's another one of our traditions: ever since I can remember, whenever my team wins, my dad makes a big deal out of letting me order ice cream. It felt special when I was nine, but now it feels a little silly, to be honest.

As I dig into a sundae, my dad asks me, "How is it?"

"It's okay, I guess."

My dad tilts his head in surprise. "Only okay?"

I don't answer. Instead, I think about how it sucks that Clay got hurt, because we're going to lose more games, and how it's good that Clay got hurt, because I'll go back to being our top scorer.

Hot fudge doesn't taste as good when you're totally confused.

CARTER

I get a ride home from Coach Benny because I'm on the way and because it gives him a chance to tell me all the things I need to work on. I half-listen and half-wonder if there's anything for dinner.

At home, I pull open the fridge door and see a few pieces of leftover chicken. I gnaw them down to the bone while staring at my backpack, with all the books and homework inside. Then I go to my room and pick up the old guitar my dad gave me for my birthday. We can't afford lessons, but I found this woman on YouTube who calls herself Patty Strums, and I learn from her. I'm not very good, to be honest, but there's something about playing guitar that is so relaxing.

Also, it's a great way to not do my homework.

Patty is in the middle of talking about barre chords—which are really hard, by the way—when my phone buzzes.

"Hey, Dad."

"Cartman?" my dad says, using the nickname he's used since before I can remember. "You sleeping, son?"

"Nah, playing guitar."

"Excellent. How was the game?"

"We lost."

"Sorry to hear it. Hey, you want to come for a ride with me? I got to pick up some stuff for work."

"Can't, Dad. Need to start my homework."

"Aw come on, Cartman, just for a little while."

I shake my head, even though he can't see it. "What kind of a father asks his son to run errands with him instead of doing his homework?"

"The kind that knows his son isn't really going to do his homework anyway."

I can't argue with him there. School isn't really my thing. But it's Eddy's thing, and he promised to help me. "Next time, Dad."

A few minutes later, I'm getting ready to head over to Eddy's house when my mom calls.

"Carter? You eat the chicken?"

"Yup. Delicious."

"Good. What are you up to?"

"Heading to Eddy's."

"To do what?"

"Homework."

"Great. Did you talk to your dad?"

"Nah." Sometimes it's just not worth telling the truth.

"Well, go to bed early. You must be exhausted."

"I have to read, like, forty pages of this book before bed."

"Forty pages? That's ridiculous. Read half of it. You need your sleep."

It's pretty hilarious. My dad wants me to drive around with him, and my mom wants me to go to bed. Neither one of them seems to care too much about my schoolwork.

No wonder my grades are lousy.

"Well, I should go, Ma," I say, but I can tell she's not quite ready to hang up.

"Have I told you recently how proud of you I am?" she asks.

"You have," I answer, but that doesn't stop her from giving her usual speech.

"You have God-given talent, Carter, and I swear, when I find myself worrying about stuff, all I have to do is think about you and how you play basketball, and it just makes me feel better about everything. Isn't that amazing?"

"It's amazing, Ma. Just like it was amazing the last ten times you told me that."

She ignores that, of course. "Coach Benny told me after the game that he thinks you can play basketball in college, maybe even get a scholarship. Isn't that wonderful, honey?"

"That would be great, Ma, but I'm in eighth grade."

I hear her sigh. "Well, yes, that's true. Okay, anyway, I'll be home late."

"Got it."

"Love you."

"Love you, too."

After we hang up, I start walking over to Eddy's, hoping he can transfer his brain into mine.

I'm pretty sure you don't have to worry about college if you fail middle school.

HEY GUYS
GREAT GAME TODAY!
EVERYONE GOOD?

KEVIN

HEY, AUSTIN. ALL GOOD

GOOD

ERIC

MY DAD SAID IT WAS ONE OF THE BEST GAMES HE EVER SAW

CHASE

WISH I COULD HAVE BEEN THERE BOYS BUT GLAD I WAS ABLE TO STIR THINGS UP THE OTHER NIGHT

ERIC

HAHAHAHA YOU GUYS KNOW I WAS NORTH4EVA RIGHT?

ANYONE TALK TO CLAY?

ERIC

I TRIED TO TEXT HIM BEFORE TO SEE HOW HE WAS DOING DIDN'T HEAR BACK

SAME

ERIC

YO PJ ARE YOU AND HIM COOL?

ME AND WHO?

ERIC

CLAY

WHAT DO YOU MEAN?

ERIC

NOTHING JUST WONDERING, AFTER THAT HALFTIME THING

YEAH WE'RE GOOD

ERIC

COOL

I MEAN, I HAVEN'T TALKED TO HIM SINCE THE GAME
BUT YEAH

CHASE

WHAT ARE YOU BOYS TALKING ABOUT?

NOTHING, I MEAN YOU HEARD CLAY GOT
HURT RIGHT?

CHASE

OF COURSE DUH

WE'RE JUST THINKING HE'S GOTTA BE SO PISSED
I MEAN WHO KNOWS HOW MANY GAMES HE'LL MISS

CHASE

IF IT'S HIS KNEE THEN THE WHOLE SEASON FOR SURE

KEVIN

THAT WOULD BEYOND SUCK

WE'LL BE OKAY WE JUST NEED TO
PICK UP THE SLACK AND PLAY HARD

ERIC

GREAT, AND ALSO WE JUST NEED SOMEONE ON OUR
TEAM TO GROW SIX INCHES BEFORE THE NEXT GAME

CHASE

HAHAHAHAHAHA

ERIC

I'D RATHER NOT THINK ABOUT IT

WHATEVER

SEE EVERYONE TOMW

WWMS
WALTHORNE SOUTH RADIO

ALFIE: Hey everyone, welcome back to Talking
                 Sports with Alfie Jenks, cool, so uh
                 today we have the captains of both
                 the girls and boys basketball teams,
                 Janeece Renfro and Carter Haswell.
                 Janeece, you have your first game
                 tonight, is that right?

JANEECE: This is so cool, Alfie. You have your
                 own radio show!

ALFIE: I know right?

JANEECE: Hey so my friend Alexa heard you
                 announcing the game the other day, she
                 said you were really good.

ALFIE: For real? That's so cool, uh, thanks,
                 well it was easy because it was such a
                 great game.

CARTER: Yeah, except for the ending.

JANEECE: I know right? That was a bummer that
                 you guys lost. We play North tonight,
                 we'll get 'em back for you.

CARTER: Oh, yeah, but I meant that kid
            getting hurt.

ALFIE: You're talking about Clay Elkind,
            center for North?

JANEECE: He's such a good player.

CARTER: Yeah he is.

JANEECE: I mean, he's no Carter Haswell, but
            he's really good.

CARTER: Ha ha. You're really good, too.

JANEECE: Thanks.

ALFIE: Hey, no flirting, this is a
            sports show!

CARTER: Ha!

ALFIE: Actually, I mentioned this to Carter
            after the game, but what's weird about
            that kid Clay is that I could see him
            limping a little bit earlier in the
            game. I was wondering if something was
            wrong with him.

CARTER: Yeah right, I was wondering the same
              thing at first, but he was so good I
              thought maybe that was, like, just how
              he ran or something.

ALFIE: With a limp?

CARTER: Whatever. I was playing the game, cut
              me some slack.

JANEECE: There was something else about that kid
              Clay that was weird too—at halftime
              I saw him, like, totally arguing with
              one of the other kids on his team.

ALFIE: Really? You saw that?

JANEECE: Yeah, I remember for sure. I was
              coming back from getting a slice of
              pizza and they were coming out of the
              locker room, like, totally yelling at
              each other.

ALFIE: Huh. Do you remember which kid?

JANEECE: Nah, I couldn't really see who the
              other kid was, the hallway was pretty
              packed, I could only see the big kid.

CARTER: That's actually not that weird. I mean
             the game was close, teammates get in
             arguments and stuff all the time. It's
             like how we get psyched up, you know?

JANEECE: Yeah duh, of course I know, I'm on
             a team, too, remember? But this was
             different. This was pretty intense.

ALFIE: Wow. Sounds like there might be a
             story there.

CARTER: What are you, like, an investigative
             reporter now?

ALFIE: Maybe. In the meantime, let's take
             some questions from our listeners.
             Please call or text your questions to
             555.284.3855.

JANEECE: How long are we supposed to wait for
             the first caller? I need to be home
             for dinner.

ALFIE: Ha ha ha.

CARTER

I don't really like to talk about basketball.

I don't like to talk about why I'm good at it, or how much I do or don't practice, or whether or not I think I can play in college or even go pro.

I don't like to talk about the fact that ever since I can remember, I just had this ability to see the court, know everything that was about to happen before it happens, or that I was born with quickness, and speed, and the ability to put the ball in the basket in a lot of different ways from a lot of different angles. And it's not like I'm bragging when I say that, because I didn't have anything to do with it. I mean, yeah I practice, but mostly I was just born with it. Kind of like how I'm already six foot two, and the doctor thinks I might get up to six-seven or six-eight. Pure luck.

Anyway, I don't like to talk about any of that stuff. I don't know why, I just don't.

Which is why, when I'm heading to lunch with Lucas, Eddy, and Sham, I kind of tune out. All they talk about is basketball, and I can't take it anymore.

Instead, I'm thinking about whether or not I was actually flirting with Janeece on Alfie's radio show—and more importantly, whether or not she was actually flirting with me—when Lucas elbows me in the ribs. "Yo Carter, what about you? You do it?"

"Do what?"

"The math homework."

I blink a few times. "Huh? I thought you guys were talking about basketball."

"We were, but now we're talking about math. Stop spacing out. You do it or not?"

"Of course I did it."

Sham laughs. "Of course you *didn't* do it, you mean."

"Oh yeah, that."

Eddy shakes his head, like he always does when I'm disappointing him, which is a lot when it comes to school. He's really smart. I'm really not. "Dude," he says, "I showed you how it worked. I practically did it for you."

"Yeah, but you didn't."

Lucas and Sham shake their heads.

"Bro, you gotta step it up a little bit," Lucas says.

"You can't fail," adds Sham.

"I swear I won't," I tell them. "I got this. I won't fail."

Suddenly I hear a different voice. "Won't fail what?"

I'm pretty sure there's only one voice that deep in the whole world. Sure enough, when I turn around, Coach Benny is standing there.

"Hey, Coach," we all say.

"Hello, boys," he rumbles. Then he repeats, "Won't fail what?"

The guys look at me, waiting.

"Uh, well Coach, math," I say. "It's really hard this quarter and I guess I am struggling a little bit. But it's all good."

"Is it, Carter? Is it all good?" Coach Benny leans into me. He smells like cologne and that unlit cigar he always has in his mouth during games. "I don't know how many times I need to tell you boys this, but basketball isn't going to make your lives better. School is going to make your lives better. Studying is going to make your lives better. Getting good grades is going to make your lives better. Planning for the future is going to make your lives better. Carter, you're one hell of a basketball player, there's no doubt about that, but even you—without school, you got nothing. You understand me?"

I nod about twelve times. "Yes, sir."

"You do?"

"I do."

"And I don't know why this needs to be said," Coach Benny adds, "but if you're having trouble with math, then get extra help. Because if you fail, you'll have some real problems, not the least of which is you won't be able to stay on the team. Any of you boys want to see that happen?"

We all say some version of "Absolutely not."

"Good," says Coach Benny. Then his eyes turn to Eddy. "You're smart at math, right?"

"I guess so," Eddy stammers.

Coach Benny gives Eddy one of his classic glares. "Don't guess. Be. And help this boy pass math." Then he walks away, leaving his cologne/cigar smell behind.

No one says anything else as we go into the cafeteria and sit down. Eventually, Eddy looks at me and says, "Well, do you understand the assignment, or not?"

I don't know why he's asking. We all know the answer.

"Uh, no," I say.

Eddy sighs, then gets out his notebook. "Fine, I'll help you. Again."

I hesitate. "Now? At lunch?"

Sham glares at me. "Are you serious? You heard what Coach Benny said. And homework is half the grade, remember?"

I pull out my notebook. As Eddy starts talking. I pretend to understand what he's talking about, but basically I just do exactly what he tells me to do.

I'm pretty sure I'm not fooling anybody.

At lunch, I sit with some of the girls from the basketball team. They're nice to me, even though they don't quite treat me as one of the gang. Which makes sense, since I'm not.

Janeece steals one of my fries. "So, Alfie. You think Carter was really flirting with me?"

"I have no idea." The last thing I want is to get in the middle of that.

"Come on!" Janeece says. "You want to be this famous reporter, right? So report!"

Another girl from the team, Callie, asks me, "Alfie, who's your best friend?"

"Um, I'm not sure?"

Callie smirks. "I know who your best friend is. Sports. Sports is your best friend, right?"

She laughs, so I laugh. "Maybe," I answer, because I don't know what else to say.

Callie and Janeece turn back to their teammates, and I look over at the next table, where Carter is eating with his pals. I notice Eddy Dixon sliding his notebook toward Carter, then

Carter opening up his own notebook and writing. Eddy might be helping him, or Carter might just be copying Eddy's homework, but before I can really tell, Janeece steals two more of my French fries.

"Hey, you guys," she announces, "Alfie thinks Carter Haswell likes me!"

I'm about to protest that's not true, but I realize no one will believe me, and all the girls are laughing, and it feels good to be a part of something, so I end up just laughing too.

5:47 pm
Clay

CLAY? HEY THIS IS ALFIE JENKS,
SPORTS REPORTER FROM WALTHORNE SOUTH.
SORRY TO DM YOU OUT OF THE BLUE
BUT I JUST WANTED TO ASK YOU A QUICK QUESTION.

CLAY?

CLAY, YOU THERE?

YEAH I'M HERE
A QUESTION ABOUT WHAT

OH HEY! THANKS FOR WRITING BACK.

WHAT'S UP

HOW ARE YOU FEELING?

NOT GREAT

OH MAN I'M SO SORRY.
YOU PLAYED SUCH A GREAT GAME THE OTHER NIGHT.
HEY, YOU KNOW I WAS JUST WONDERING, I THOUGHT I NOTICED YOU LIMPING EARLIER IN THE GAME,
WERE YOU HURT?

NAH I WAS FINE

OH OKAY COOL.
BUT IT JUST SEEMED LIKE YOU WERE LIMPING A LITTLE,
EVEN THOUGH YOU WERE PLAYING TOTALLY AMAZING,
I MEAN HOLY MOLY YOU WERE LIGHTING IT UP

THANKS

SO YOU WEREN'T HURT BEFORE?

YOU ASKED ME THAT ALREADY LIKE THREE TIMES

I KNOW I'M SORRY I WAS JUST WONDERING

CLAY YOU STILL THERE?

CLAY?

I DON'T KNOW, I GOT A LITTLE BANGED UP AT PRACTICE

JEEZ I THOUGHT SO
HOW BAD

NOT THAT BAD

BUT YOU DECIDED TO PLAY ANYWAY?

YEAH IT WAS A BIG GAME

WHY DID YOU PLAY?
WAS IT YOUR IDEA OR DID SOMEONE TALK YOU
INTO IT?

WHAT IS THIS, LAW AND ORDER?

HAHAHA NO NO NO
I'M JUST TRYING TO GET THE STORY.
MR. RASHAD SAYS ALWAYS GET THE STORY

WHO?

NEVER MIND, THAT WAS DUMB,
SO YOU'RE SAYING YOU DIDN'T FEEL ANY PRESSURE
TO PLAY?
I MEAN, BECAUSE OBVIOUSLY YOU'RE THE
BEST PLAYER
AND IT WAS THE FIRST GAME OF THE SEASON
AGAINST YOUR ARCH RIVALS!

NAH
I MEAN, I GUESS MAYBE A LITTLE

WAS IT THE COACH?
IS YOUR COACH SUPER INTENSE?
I HEARD YOU WERE ARGUING WITH ONE OF YOUR
TEAMMATES AT HALFTIME,
WAS HE TELLING YOU NOT TO PLAY?
WAS HE TELLING YOU NOT TO LISTEN TO
THE COACH?

NOT EXACTLY
I GOTTA GO

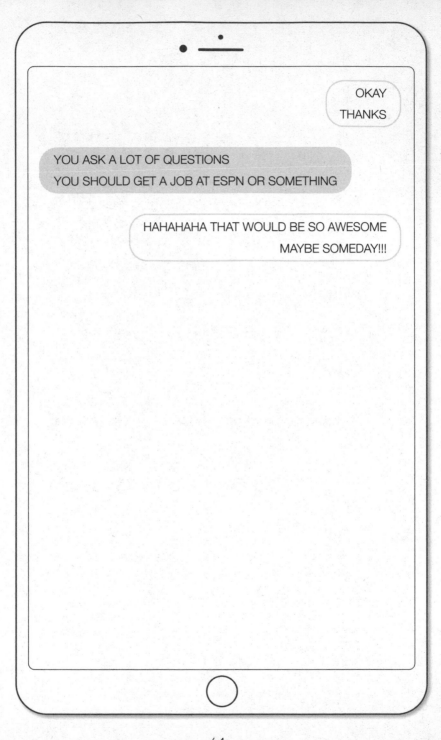

OKAY

THANKS

YOU ASK A LOT OF QUESTIONS

YOU SHOULD GET A JOB AT ESPN OR SOMETHING

HAHAHAHA THAT WOULD BE SO AWESOME

MAYBE SOMEDAY!!!

AUSTIN

When I was ten, and my younger sister, Liv, was eight, my parents got us a private basketball coach named Mr. Cashen.

"Call me Coach Cash," he said, so we did.

Coach Cash played in college with my dad and ran basketball summer camps for some sneaker company, so he was kind of a big deal. And he was a great coach. He taught us shooting technique, ball handling, how to defend the pick-and-roll, what pass to throw in what situation, the best way to box out under the basket.

He taught us everything but height and speed.

It turned out my little sister didn't need to be taught either one of those—Liv was really tall for a girl and super quick. So after the first few weeks of lessons, my dad said to Coach Cash, "We'll do two sessions a week for Austin, and one for Liv. He's going to need the extra help."

You would have thought that my dad would have said that in private, but nope. I was standing right there.

Ever since then, Coach Cash has been pretty tough on me.

His favorite word is "again."

Actually, I take that back.

His favorite word is "AGAIN!"

"AGAIN!" he'd yell, after I'd taken fifty foul shots.

"AGAIN!" he'd yell, after I'd dribbled a basketball in each hand up and down the court a hundred times.

"AGAIN!" he'd yell, after I ran suicide sprints for fifteen minutes.

"AGAIN!" he'd yell, after I ran backward from foul line to foul line ten times.

So I'd do it again, and again, and again, and again. And at first I was happy to do it, because I got a lot better, and I loved the game.

But as I got older, I stopped getting a lot better and started getting only a little better. And before too long, it got to the point where I never wanted to hear the word "again" again.

No such luck.

"AGAIN!"

We're at the Tompkins Park courts a few days after we beat South. Coach Cash was at the game, and he didn't like the way I was distributing the ball on the fast break, so he's making me dribble up and down the court at a dead sprint while he yells, "LEFT! RIGHT! LEFT! RIGHT!" I'm supposed to turn my head in whatever direction he calls, which is how I work on knowing where my teammates are while going at full speed.

"Good," Coach Cash says, after we've been doing this for about ten minutes. "Much better."

I take that to mean we're on a break, and I head for the sideline.

"Where ya goin'? We're not done. AGAIN!"

Finally, after another fifteen minutes and I'm on the verge of collapse, it's time for a water break. I'm sitting on the bench, sucking major wind, when Coach Cash takes a seat next to me.

"Good work today. You're getting it. Now listen, I got news."

For a brief second, I think he's going to tell me he's moving somewhere far away, like Australia, and my heart fills with hope.

"I'm starting a new program, and I want you to be a part of it."

"Awesome!" I say, trying to mean it. "What kind of program?"

"It's an invitation-only AAU program called Slam Academy, and I'm pulling in some of the best players in the state," Coach Cash tells me. "We're going to have a high school team and a junior team. I'd like you to join the juniors."

I make myself sound as excited as possible. "Wow. That's so cool. You want me on the team?"

"Of course I want you on the team. You can really play!"

Remember how I said you can't teach height and speed? Well, it turns out you also can't teach having a dad who was a college teammate of the guy who's starting the team.

Coach Cash blows his whistle, which is pretty unnecessary, since we're the only two people there. "Up and at 'em! Time for some box-out drills! Let's go!"

I stand under the hoop while he throws up intentionally missed shot after intentionally missed shot, which I attempt to rebound. He pushes me from behind while firing out instructions. "No elbows! Use your butt! Grab the ball with both hands! Keep it up high!"

So I don't use my elbows, and I use my butt, and I grab the ball with both hands, and I keep it high.

"HIGHER! AGAIN!"

"DON'T FLAIL! AGAIN!"

"EYES DOWNCOURT! AGAIN!"

Every time I do it AGAIN, it feels like I'm messing up more, not less. And then it hits me: I've finally reached the point where the more Coach Cash tells me to do something, the worse I get at it.

The good news is, Coach Cash is paid to tell me what to do for only an hour at a time. So today, after the hour is up, he blows his whistle again. "Great work!" he barks, which is kind of funny, since he's spent the last sixty minutes telling me everything I was doing wrong. "See you Thursday."

Can't wait.

We shake hands, he leaves, and I sit there, looking down at the basketball in my hands.

You and I used to be such good friends, I tell the ball. *What happened?*

My self-pity party is broken up by a voice behind me. "Yo!"

I turn around to see Kevin, Eric, and a few other guys from the team heading my way. I remember that I'd told them to come meet me here for a pickup game.

"Let's run a few games," Eric says, as we slap hands.

"I don't know. I'm pretty sore from my workout."

Kevin waves me off. "Get out with that," he says. "Come on, let's ball."

"Aight," I say to Kevin.

He looks at me and raises his eyebrows. "'Aight'?" he repeats. He always calls me out when I talk differently to him, because he's the one Black kid on our team. He's totally right, of course.

"I mean yeah, let's go for it," I say.

We start the game, and on the first play I crossover Eric and hit a reverse scoop layup.

"All day!" I holler at Eric.

"Last time!" he hollers back.

We play for ninety minutes, and no one yells "AGAIN!" once.

And just like that, I remember why basketball is the greatest game in the world.

My dad was hoping I would be a boy. He was okay with me being a girl, though, because I was their first child, and he probably thought he and my mom were going to have a lot more kids.

But they ended up having zero more kids, so I was it.

Everyone's heard this type of story before, about the sports-crazed dad who doesn't have any sons, so he transfers all his sports craziness onto his daughter. In my version of the story, it took only about two minutes in first grade for me to realize I was *terrible* at sports. It took my dad a little longer, though—about ten minutes.

But here's the funny thing: I love sports.

LOVE them.

And it was my mom, who used to write for her high school newspaper, who told me that I could still be very involved with sports, even if I was the least-coordinated person ever born. Because I could follow sports. I could study them. And when I was old enough, I could cover them, and talk about them, and write about them, and report on them, and even announce them.

So that's what I did.

And that's what I do.

When I was ten, I wrote an article about the kickball tournament we had in fifth grade, when Louis Benson's team beat Alice Freehold's team 28–27 in a real thriller. My parents said the article was great. My dad said, "It's almost like I was there!"

I was so happy when he said that.

Then, when I got to Walthorne South, I met Mr. Rashad. He's a guidance counselor, and also the media advisor, which basically meant that he was going to be the most important person in my life for the next three years.

But our school doesn't have the greatest media department. We don't have a lot of money for that kind of stuff. In fact, we don't have ANY money for that kind of stuff. But we do have a microphone and a transmitter. I don't know what a transmitter does or how it works exactly—Mr. Rashad handles that part— but when I was in sixth grade, he let me hold the microphone, and he showed me the transmitter, and he told me, "You know what this is? This is a radio station."

A RADIO STATION!

Right then and there I knew what I was going to do. "I am going to write about sports for the school newspaper," I told him, "and blog about sports for the town website, and talk about sports on the school radio station."

"So you want to be a journalist?"

I nodded. "A journalist about sports, yes."

"That's great. If you're going to be a journalist, you must care about one thing, and one thing only."

"Sports?"

Mr. Rashad shook his head. "Truth. The truth is the only thing that matters."

"The truth is the only thing that matters," I repeated.

Mr. Rashad smiled again.

"Welcome to WWMS."

PROWLING WITH THE PANTHERS
A MIDDLE SCHOOL SPORTS BLOG BY ALFIE JENKS
WEDNESDAY, NOVEMBER 14

Injured Player: What Really Happened?

Hi again everyone, it's Alfie, back to talk (well, actually write about) sports. Thanks a lot for reading my blog! Last night, the Walthorne South Panthers boys basketball team evened their record at 1 and 1 by beating the Harborville Boaters, 59–43.

Carter Haswell led the scoring as usual, with 26 points. The girls team tries to make it two in a row when they play Ackton tonight. Meanwhile, across town, the Walthorne North boys team played their first game without star center Clay Elkind and lost 54–49 to Suffolk Central.

Speaking of Clay Elkind, he really played an incredible game against Walthorne North last week—he led their team in scoring and rebounding and was clearly their best player. But the amazing thing was, he did all this even though he seemed to be limping through most of the game.

Then, just before the end of the game, Clay made a game-saving play but landed awkwardly. The whole gym held its breath as he screamed in agony, lying on the floor until his coaches helped him to the bench. And from what I'm hearing, he may be out for the season.

I checked in with Clay earlier this week, and he didn't really want to talk about the injury, but he did tell me he came into the game already hurt. It's hard to know exactly what happened here, but I have a pretty good guess. It was the first game of the season, against a big rival. Somebody, probably his coach or maybe even his parents, pressured Clay to play, told him how important he was to the team and what a big moment it was, and how everyone was counting on him. And then he gave in to the pressure and played, and then, well, you know the rest.

It's really too bad. I hope Clay has a speedy recovery. I hope he can play basketball again up to his very high level, because he's a really incredible player. And it would be great to see him on the court again by the time North meets South in the last game of the season. That would sure be a great comeback story!

THURSDAY, NOVEMBER 15 2:36 PM

Young Reporter Causes Stir with Blog Post

The youth sports community in Walthorne is buzzing today, after a blog post last night by Walthorne South Middle School eighth grader Alfie Jenks suggested that a young athlete was pressured to play while hurt, which may have led to his severe injury late in the game.

Referring to last Friday night's contest between Walthorne South and Walthorne North, Ms. Jenks implies that starting North center Clay Elkind was convinced by adults, possibly a coach, to stay on the court even though he was obviously limping. Later in the game, young Mr. Elkind suffered ligament damage in his knee and had to be carried off the court.

In a combined statement this morning, the physical education departments of both schools said, "While we appreciate young Ms. Jenks's zeal for a good story, there is absolutely no truth to the innuendo that any coach, or anyone in any official capacity, urged this young player to compete in a game despite being injured. Our athletic programs are focused solely on participation, personal growth, and the invaluable experience that comes from being part of a team. It may be true that youth sports, like many student activities, occasionally reach an inappropriate level of pressure, but please be assured that we take our Walthorne tradition of courtesy, cooperation, and fair play very seriously and believe in it deeply."

Walthornenews.com reached out to the coaches of Walthorne South and Walthorne North Middle Schools with follow-up questions, but both were unavailable for comment.

YO ALFIE, WHY DID YOU DO THAT

DO WHAT?

WRITE THAT ARTICLE ABOUT ME

WHAT DO YOU MEAN? WE TALKED ABOUT IT.
IT WAS ON THE RECORD.

I DON'T EVEN KNOW WHAT THAT MEANS

IT MEANS IT WAS A PÙBLIC CONVERSATION

WHATEVER
ALL I KNOW IS YOU ASKED ME A FEW QUESTIONS
AND NOW IT'S LIKE LOCAL NEWS OR SOMETHING

YIKES CLAY
I HOPE YOU'RE NOT MAD
I DON'T THINK IT MAKES YOU LOOK BAD
OR ANYTHING
YOU'RE THE VICTIM HERE, RIGHT??

BUT YOU GOT IT WRONG

WHAT DO YOU MEAN

WHAT YOU WROTE
THAT'S NOT WHAT HAPPENED

WHAT DO YOU MEAN

NEVER MIND
JUST DON'T WRITE ABOUT ME AGAIN OKAY?

HOLD ON
WHAT PART DID I GET WRONG?

CLAY?

CLAY ARE YOU THERE??

Friday at 4:59 pm

Lucas Just want to offer Alfie Jenks some props for her blog, nicely done

Like · Reply

Friday at 5:03 pm

Carter That's pretty bogus
No coach should make a kid play hurt

Like · Reply

Friday at 5:06 pm

Janeece If it's true then that coach should be fired tbh

Like · Reply

Friday at 5:09 pm

Sham What do you mean if

Like · Reply

Friday at 5:13 pm

Janeece Well we don't know for sure

Like · Reply

Friday at 5:16 pm

Alfie Guys Janeece is right, I probably shouldn't have written that part about the coach

Like · Reply

Friday at 5:17 pm

Carter Cmon we all know that dude was hurting before he got injured

Like · Reply

Friday at 5:19 pm

Alfie Yeah okay fine but we don't know the details and Clay never said it was the coach who told him he should play

Like · Reply

Friday at 5:21 pm

Briscoe Who was it then

Like · Reply

Friday at 5:22 pm

Alfie I don't know

Like · Reply

Friday at 5:24pm

Lucas North guys you out there? Fill us in

Like · Reply

Friday at 5:26 pm

North4Eva Yeah I'm here and you guys don't know what you're talking about and it's none of your business and whoever Alfie Jenks is really needs to back off

Like · Reply

Friday at 5:28 pm

Carter Whoa dude calm down
And why don't you stop hiding behind an anonymous handle for starters

Like · Reply

Friday at 5:30 pm

North4Eva I'm not hiding
my name is Eric

Like · Reply

Friday at 5:33 pm

Sham Okay Eric well maybe you shouldn't worry about what is and isn't people's business

Like · Reply

Friday at 5:35 pm

Clay This is ridiculous everyone should just stop
None of you know what happened

Like · Reply

Friday at 5:36 pm

Sham Okay what happened then

Like · Reply

Friday at 5:38 pm

Kevin What happened is we beaaaaat yooouuuuuuu

Like · Reply

Friday at 5:39 pm

North4Eva Hahahahahahah

Like · Reply

Friday at 5:40 pm

Lucas Enjoy it while it lasts

Like · Reply

Friday at 5:43 pm

North4Eva I'm enjoying it almost as much as you guys enjoy that free lunch you get over there

Like · Reply

Friday at 5:45 pm

Sham you better back off son before I knock that smug grin off your rich boy face

Like · Reply

Friday at 5:47 pm

Kevin Easy fellas

Like · Reply

Friday at 5:49 pm

Janeece Everyone knock it off or they're gonna take this thread down

Like · Reply

Friday at 5:51 pm

Chase This is so fun I'm loving every minute of it
#betterthannetflix
#freelunchforthepoorkids

Like · Reply

Friday at 5:53 pm

Austin Seriously?

Honestly you guys this is pathetic

You want to know what happened with Clay?

I'll tell you

It was me

I'm the one who pressured him to play

Clay hurt his ankle earlier in the week in practice and was limping. I knew he was injured, everyone knew he was injured, but I'm the captain, and I wanted to beat South. I knew we needed him, so I begged him to play. All week. And he didn't want to play. But I talked him into it. And before the game Coach Zirkusky asked Clay how he felt and he said fine, and I don't know what Clay's parents thought about him playing but they definitely didn't say he couldn't play, so the day of the game I asked him one last time and he said he was going to play. And in the first half he played great and I could tell he was hurting but it didn't seem to be affecting his game, but then at halftime Clay came to me and said he thought he was done, the leg didn't feel right, and I kind of went nuts. I admit it, I freaked out. I said this is gonna be the hardest game we play all year and we just needed him for one more half, he could sit the next game if it didn't feel right, and so we got into it, yelling, and the coach came over and asked what we were fighting about, and I didn't say anything, and Clay didn't say anything, and the coach asked if we were ready to roll for the second half, and I looked at Clay, and he said let's do it, and he played great but got hurt, and yeah I feel like crap about it.

So that's what happened and it would be great if everyone would just stop talking about it.

Like · Reply

Friday at 6:09 pm

Carter Sorry man that's tough
Hang in there
How's Clay

Like · Reply

Friday at 6:12 pm

Austin Pretty sure he's out for the season
And it's all because of me

Like · Reply

Friday at 6:14 pm

Carter Don't blame yourself dude
Seriously

Like · Reply

Friday at 6:16 pm

Austin Carter I appreciate that
But whatever
I just gotta learn to live with it
And now I'm signing off and like I said everyone can stop talking
about it

Like · Reply

ALFIE

I stare at Austin's words, not quite understanding, then totally understanding.

I messed up, big time.

I'm supposed to find the truth, and instead, I guessed the truth.

And I guessed wrong.

I turn my phone off, turn my computer off, and bury my face in my hands.

I'm embarrassed and ashamed.

And I vow never to make the same mistake again.

As if laying it all out there online isn't stressful enough, now it's time for Friday family dinner.

Friday family dinner is a big deal in my house.

During the week, my dad is either traveling for work or gets home late, and on Saturdays and Sundays we usually have sports or other activities or my parents go out, but on Friday nights we eat together at 7:30 sharp.

Liv and I alternate nights setting the table, and tonight it's my night. As I'm putting the forks down, Liv shows me something on her phone. It's a meme she found online, a picture of Clay lying on the ground and screaming in pain and me leaning over him to see if he's okay.

And on the picture someone has written, DUDE! PRACTICE TOMORROW, 9 AM SHARP!

I wave Liv away. "Get that thing out of my face."

We all sit down. For the first few minutes, as usual, no one says anything except stuff like *Pass the steak* and *Do you have enough water?* and *Make sure to take some broccoli.* Then there's a few minutes of quiet eating, while we wait for my dad to start a conversation about basketball.

I eat, and wait.

The first thing we talk about is Liv's travel league game from the night before. She was the leading scorer, as usual.

"I played okay, I guess," Liv says, even though she knows she played great.

"That's an understatement," my mom says.

My dad nods. "You're looking really strong out there, Liv. Really strong. Maybe work on your free throws a bit, but otherwise, no complaints."

No complaints from my dad is like *You're the greatest thing since sliced bread* from anyone else.

Liv beams. "I worked on my foul shooting today, Dad. I went 39 for 50."

"Good for you, kiddo."

I have an urge to roll my eyes, but I manage not to.

My dad's phone buzzes. He glances at it and reads something quickly. Then he looks up, right at me.

"This is the third text I've gotten tonight from a parent asking how you're doing. What's this about?"

I hold his gaze for a few seconds, then look down at my plate. "I told some people that I was the one who talked Clay into playing even though he was hurt."

My dad scoffs. "Yeah well, his injury has nothing to do with you. It's a freak thing that happened. Nobody's fault. Certainly not yours."

He says it in a way that means we're done with that topic. But for some reason, I decide I'm not done. "Actually, Dad, it kind of was somebody's fault."

Silverware stops clinking.

"Is that right?" my dad asks. "Whose fault was it then?"

"Uh, mine. Like I said, I made Clay play, knowing he was already hurt."

"You didn't make him play. It was his decision."

"I'm the captain."

My dad takes a long sip of water. "The coach would have held him out if he thought Clay was in danger of further injury. Not your call."

It's obvious we're not getting anywhere, so I stop talking.

"It's a complicated situation, Austin," my mom chimes in. She's trying to make peace, as usual. "I mean, you can't be expected to have the judgment of an adult. I understand that you might feel bad, but saying that you are responsible for Clay's injury is just ridiculous."

I feel more comfortable with my mom, so I direct my answer to her. "It's not that complicated, actually. I wanted to win, and the best chance we had to win was by me talking Clay into playing. Now he's hurt, so obviously that was a dumb idea, because we're not going to win nearly as many games with him out."

"Well, at least you'll get the ball a lot more," my dad says. "Like I said at Currier's, I'll be shocked if your scoring average doesn't go way up, since you're going to be seeing a lot more of the ball."

"I guess," I say, trying not to feel guilty about it. "My shooting percentage should go way up, too."

"Exactly!" My dad nods, satisfied that we can agree on something. Which is my mom's cue to change the subject.

"Do you guys want to talk about our spring break plans?" she asks.

"SWEEEET!" says Liv, grinning from ear to ear.

"Well, this year we thought we'd try something different," my mom says. "I mean, no one loves lying in the sun more than me, but we don't always need to be so lazy. And besides, there's so much great stuff to see in our very own amazing country, right you guys?"

I notice my sister's grin has faded a little bit.

My mom gives us her biggest, happiest smile—maybe a little too big and happy. "So, your dad and I decided we're all going to go to Wyoming to do some camping, and some hiking and fishing, and see all the amazing wildlife at Yellowstone National Park. Bears and moose and wolves! How's that sound?"

"We're still working out the details, depending on when the league playoffs end," my dad adds.

My sister starts playing with her hair, which she always does when she decides to pout about something. "So wait, are we gonna, like, sleep in a tent and stuff?"

"For a few nights, yes," says my dad. "We'll also be in a lodge. But if you're expecting pancake breakfasts and video games and hair salons, well, it's not that kind of vacation. We're going to be roughing it a little bit, for a change."

"Okay, yeah, sounds amazing," Liv says, sounding unamazed. "But . . . can we go back to the Caribbean at Christmas?"

My dad sighs, then finally looks at me. "What about you, Austin? You think it sounds fun?"

I don't answer right away. Instead, my mind flashes back to the chain from the night before, when Eric made that gross "free lunch" joke about the guys at South, and Chase turned it into a hashtag. Then I think of Carter Haswell telling me to hang in there. I wonder what he would think about going to Wyoming and "roughing it."

I look at my dad.

"It sounds fantastic," I say. "May I be excused?"

While I wait for my mom to get home from work and drive me over to Dad's, I have my usual argument with myself: Should I practice guitar or basketball? The truth is, I'd rather play guitar, but I feel guilty if I don't work on my game.

So I decide to do both.

I go out to the hoop behind my apartment building and start working on my left hand. Everyone has a strong side, and I'm a natural rightie, but if you're going to be good at any sport, you have to learn how to use both hands or both feet. I'm lucky because I'm kind of ambidextrous to begin with, and I invented this little game where I throw the ball up against the backboard and rebound it and put it back up with my left hand. I tell myself that once I make fifty shots in a row, I can go inside and turn on Patty Strums. She just released a video called "The Four Chords That Will Make You a Guitar God," and I really want to check it out.

Unfortunately, I'm only up to thirty-two in a row by the time my mom drives up. Becoming a guitar god will have to wait.

"MA!" I whine. "You're early!"

She looks at her watch. "Not according to mama time I'm not. I've gotta drop you off and be back at work by six, so let's get a move on."

My mom's car kind of sounds like a hippopotamus with asthma, so we have to shout at each other while she's driving.

"I GOT AN INTERESTING PHONE CALL TODAY," she shouts.

"FROM WHO?"

"FROM SOME COACH. HE SAID COACH BENNY GAVE HIM MY NUMBER, AND HE'S STARTING A FANCY BASKETBALL TEAM AND HE WANTS YOU TO BE ON IT. THE FIRST PRACTICE IS NEXT TUESDAY. PRETTY COOL, HUH?"

"WHAT KIND OF TEAM?"

"I FORGET EXACTLY. UAA? AUU?"

"AAU?"

"YUP THAT'S THE ONE!"

Whoa. I've heard about AAU. That's where the real basketball is played.

"HOLY MOLY."

"I KNOW!"

We don't talk much after that, partly because I'm suddenly in my own world thinking about real basketball, and partly because it gets tiring shouting in the car.

My mom drops me off at some house my dad is painting. "HAVE FUN!" she hollers. "DON'T LET HIM MAKE YOU DO ALL THE WORK AS USUAL."

I find my dad around the back, up on a ladder, doing some window trim work. He sees me and backs down the ladder slowly and carefully, which he's done ever since he had a bad spill and hurt his back a few years ago.

"Cartman," he says. "Ready to work?"

"Mom says you're not supposed to ask me that."

My dad laughs. "Still telling me what to do."

He hands me four paint brushes and a bucket of water, and I do what I always do, which is rinse them out and dry them. My dad would never let me do any actual painting, of course. He just has me do the stuff he doesn't want to do. Can't say that I blame him.

After about twenty minutes, I ask my dad my favorite question: "Break time?"

"Sure. I'm a little bit ahead on this job, anyway."

As we sit on the back of my dad's truck, my dad turns his body away from me, then takes a little bottle of something and pours it into his coffee. He doesn't think I see this, but I do. I've seen him do it for years, and I know exactly what's happening. But I've never asked him about it.

Instead, I take a sip of juice, then tell him the news: "So Dad, some guy called mom today, and asked if I would join this AAU basketball team. I guess it starts next week."

My dad raises an eyebrow. "AAU? What's that stand for?"

"I'm not sure, but it's, like, this league that only takes the best players."

"Whoa," my dad says. "Sounds expensive."

I'm not surprised by his response. With my dad, everything comes down to money. Probably because he's never had any.

"I don't know about that."

He takes a swig of his special coffee. "So you don't know how much it costs?"

"No, Dad. I don't even know who the guy is. Mom talked to him."

"Aha. Well, anything for her little boy, even if it means spending money we don't got."

And that pretty much explains why my parents aren't married anymore.

"You don't even know that it costs money, Dad."

"Everything costs money."

I check the time on my phone. I have a sudden urge to be anywhere else.

"Listen," my dad says. "I know how the world works. There are a lot of people out there who are happy to pay a lot of money to make sure little Johnny or little Jenny gets the best of everything. Especially when it comes to sports."

"So you're saying I can't play?"

"Not saying that at all." He finishes the last of his drink. "You're a real good player, Cartman. You got something special, and people want kids with something special. So you join this team, and you show them how badly they need you. You play so well that they wouldn't dream of making you pay. You make sure you're the best player on the team. And then you keep making sure you're the best, right through high school, all the way 'til the day some college coach says, 'How'd you like a free college education? All you have to do is shoot that ball in that basket for a few years.' And then who knows, if you work hard enough, you might even make it to the NBA, and I can stop falling off ladders, and your mom can stop doing double shifts all week. All you have to do is be the very best, every step of the way, starting with this AAU thing." He winks at me. "Easy peasy, right?"

"Ha," I say, squinting up into the sunshine.

My dad jumps off the truck. "And speaking of being the best," he says, "I'm the best housepainter in this whole town, and I start on a new job next week, so I need to finish this up today."

As I watch him paint, one thought keeps going through my head.

I guess I start a new job next week, too.

AUSTIN

Clay's not answering any of my texts, so over the weekend I decide to just show up at his house.

His mom answers the door. "Austin! Hello." She looks surprised to see me. And not necessarily in a good way.

"Hi, Ms. Elkind. Is Clay home?"

"He's in his room, go ahead up."

I take the stairs two at a time and knock on Clay's door.

"Who is it?"

"Austin."

Five-second pause.

"Come in."

Clay is lying on his bed, staring at his phone, his left leg up on a few pillows.

"What's up," he says.

"Not much. I've been texting you."

"Yeah, sorry, got a lot going on."

I'm not sure what that could be since he's laid up in bed, but I'm not going to say that out loud. "So, how's it going? What'd the doctor say?"

"Some ligament damage, but not torn. Out for six to eight weeks at least. But there's a chance I can play again this season."

"That's great news!"

"Yeah, fantastic."

I take a deep breath and stare out the window at his pool, which is covered up for the season. "Listen, dude. I don't know what to say. I messed up. I'm sorry."

He's still staring at his phone. "Yeah, no, it's cool." But it doesn't seem cool.

"We're gonna really miss you out there, Clay. You're our best player and everyone knows it."

"Not anymore. Order has been restored to the universe."

"What does that mean?"

He looks up at me for the first time. "It means that for a long time, you were the best player. Then I grew tall and developed my game, and all of a sudden I was really good. Maybe even better than you. But now that I'm hurt, you're the man again. Like I said, order has been restored to the universe."

"Bro, you're being ridiculous. I don't care about being 'the man.' I just want to win."

"Come on, PJ." Clay adjusts one of the pillows under his leg. "Isn't there some small part of you that's psyched to be the leading scorer again? I mean, think about it—you're part of the most famous basketball family in Walthorne. Now your parents won't freak out that their son is the second-best player."

I shake my head. "Seriously? Come on."

Clay hesitates, like he's not sure he wants to say what he's about to say, but he says it, anyway. "Listen, I hate to say this, man, and I don't believe it myself, but I've heard some people talking about how, like, maybe you wanted me to get injured, so you could take over the team again."

I can't believe what I'm hearing. "What? Are you for real right now? Like who?"

"I mean, you did kind of pressure me to play hurt, right?"

My skin starts to prickle, like it's on fire. "Listen, Clay. I feel really bad that you got hurt, but it's not like I ordered you to play the other night, I just asked you to." I hear how mad I sound, and I don't like it, but I can't help it. "The coach could have told you not to. Your mom and dad could have told you not to. And also, you might have gotten that injury at the end of the game even if you hadn't been hurt before. Injuries happen all the time in sports, remember? That's part of the deal. So whatever you're hearing is bull, and you know it. Whatever. I'm gonna go."

I start to walk out of his room, then turn around and poke my head back in. "I hope you feel better," I say.

Then I run down the stairs and out the front door without saying goodbye to his mom.

WWMS
WALTHORNE SOUTH RADIO

ALFIE: Hello, and welcome to Talking Sports
                on WWMS. My name is Alfie Jenks. My
                guest today is Mr. Rashad, who works
                as a counselor in the Walthorne School
                System. Mr. Rashad, thank you very
                much for joining us today.

MR. RASHAD: Wow, Alfie, you sound very professional.

ALFIE: I'm not, trust me.

MR. RASHAD: Well, I'm impressed.

ALFIE: Thank you! I have asked Mr. Rashad
                to join us today to discuss youth
                sports and the situation regarding the
                blog post I wrote, when I mistakenly
                suggested that the coach of Walthorne
                North told one of his players, Clay
                Elkind, to play hurt.

MR. RASHAD: Yes, I heard about that.

ALFIE: I feel horrible and I promise to never
                make a mistake like that again, but

what do you think about the fact that
Clay was playing in the game?

MR. RASHAD: I think it's good that you're going to
be more careful about your reporting
from now on. As for that young man
who was playing hurt, I wish I could
say I was surprised, but I'm not. I've
seen all sorts of things happen on the
field of play—or the court, in this
instance—that make me wonder if the
whole business of youth sports hasn't
gotten a little cockeyed.

ALFIE: Cockeyed? How so?

MR. RASHAD: Well, for one thing, I know that
another player on Clay's team took
responsibility for urging Clay to play
when he was injured. But when it comes
to these kinds of decisions, it's not
the player's fault. It's never the
player's fault.

ALFIE: I'm not sure what you mean, Mr.
Rashad. Can you explain?

MR. RASHAD: Sure, Alfie. The young man at Walthorne
North who was encouraging his teammate

to play through an injury may not have
been using his best judgment. But in
these types of situations, it's always
up to the adults to make sure the very
best judgment is used, and in this
case they failed. That is my concern,
Alfie: It's those very adults that get
so caught up in the need to win, and
being the best, that sometimes they
forget their main responsibility,
which is to protect the youngsters and
allow them to grow.

ALFIE: Huh. Well, that makes a ton of sense.

MR. RASHAD: The thing is, Alfie, we can't just
               complain about it. We also have to ask
               ourselves: Is there anything we can do
               about it?

ALFIE: I sure hope so. Well, thanks for
               coming on my show, Mr. Rashad. This
               has been Alfie Jenks, Talking Spor—
               wait, actually, hold on a second! We
               have a caller! My first caller ever!
               This is so exciting!

MR. RASHAD: Congratulations. You might want to
               answer it.

ALFIE: Oh yeah, right! Uh, hello? You're
                on the air with Alfie Jenks,
                Talking Sports.

CALLER: Oh, hey. Uh, yeah, listen, I don't
                have a question or anything. I
                just, uh, want to say I agree with
                everything you guys are saying and
                well, there's another thing you guys
                should know about, and that is there's
                this girl who goes to Walthorne North
                who's like a star athlete, and uh, she
                moved to another town over the summer
                but still goes to Walthorne North
                just so she can play on the basketball
                team. Is that legal?

ALFIE: Whoa.

MR. RASHAD: Who is calling, please?

CALLER: Uh, I'd rather not say.

ALFIE: It's a good question—is that legal,
                Mr. Rashad?

MR. RASHAD: Well, actually if what you're saying
                is true, and there hasn't been
                specific permission granted for

some extenuating reason, then no,
it's not.

ALFIE: Are you sure you don't want to give
                us your name? (PAUSE) Hello? Hello? I
                think they hung up.

MR. RASHAD: I think they may have.

ALFIE: Well, that sure is an interesting way
                to end the show. My guest has been
                guidance counselor and media advisor
                Mr. Rashad. This is Alfie Jenks,
                Talking Sports—well actually, talking
                about what's wrong with sports. Thanks
                for listening.

CARTER

A few days after my dad telling me that all I have to do to solve our problems is become a superstar in the NBA, I'm heading home after practice with Eddy. We walk together pretty much every day, since we live in the same neighborhood. Usually, we talk about fun stuff, like is this TV show better than that TV show, or what song we're obsessed with, but today, we're talking about the opposite of fun stuff. We're talking about math. More specifically, the test we have coming up later in the week.

"No, man, I keep telling you," Eddy says. "To figure out the percentage of the number Y that X represents, you have to divide X by Y, then multiply the result by a hundred."

I try to roll that around in my brain, but it just makes my head hurt. "Got it," I tell Eddy, hoping he'll believe me. He doesn't.

"Dude, you just need to pass," he says. "You need to get sixty percent. That means sixty percent out of what number?"

"Uh, seventy?" I say. He responds by punching my arm.

When we get to my building, I notice something weird right away: My dad's truck is parked out front, right behind my mom's car. This never happens. I can't remember the last time my parents were in the same room without me.

"Huh," I say, pointing at the truck.

Eddy sees it and whistles. "What's up with that?"

"I have no idea."

We high-five our goodbyes and I head up the stairs, since the elevator's out again. It's five flights, so I'm totally out of breath by the time I walk into our apartment. My mom and my dad are sitting together at the kitchen table, looking like someone's cat just died.

My mom gets up and walks over to me. "How was practice?" she asks.

"Fine," I pant, still out of breath from the stairs.

She glances at my dad, then back at me. "Something happened with your father today," she says. "Something at work."

"What?"

"I'll let him tell you."

My dad stares straight ahead, holding a beer in his hand. I notice he keeps clenching his hands into fists. I recognize this from the old days, when he would get mad at my mom and try to keep his anger under control. Almost always, he succeeded. Every once in a while, he didn't.

"I had an incident at work today," he says, so softly I can barely hear him. "I started this new job, and the lady seemed nice enough, but she wanted me to paint this section of a wall that was right near some fancy sculpture of an eagle or something. I told her I needed to move the sculpture, but she said it couldn't move under any circumstances because it was really valuable and only a professional mover could move it, and she said that I should just be careful, and I said of course, I'm always careful, but then as I'm painting, one of my brushes starts to slide off the tray, I don't know how, I mean that's never happened before, and as I reach for it I guess I nudged the dang thing a little bit, the sculpture of the eagle I mean, and it fell and got chipped."

He pauses, and I say the first thing that pops into my head. "Were you drunk?"

My dad looks shocked, then angry. "What? No! Of course not! Why would you ask that?"

"Because you're always drinking, Dad. You don't think I notice, but I do." I point at his beer. "Look, you're drinking right now."

"We all do what we need to do to get through the day. But I'm never drunk on the job." He looks at my mom for help.

"This isn't about that," she says, quietly.

"Not at all," my dad says.

I've never heard my dad talk like this before. He sounds scared.

"Well, it doesn't really sound like it was your fault, Dad," I tell him. "I mean, you told her you needed to move the sculpture, right? She's not blaming you, is she?"

His eyes look sad. Lost. "You gotta understand something about how the world works, Carter," he says. "When the homeowner says one thing and the housepainter says another, the homeowner is always right."

My dad gets up without another word and walks into the other room. I look at my mom, who makes a face like, *I wouldn't go in there right now if I were you.*

So I sit at the kitchen table. My mom sits down next to me.

"Apparently your dad argued with the woman, and she told him to leave," she says. "Then she called Rico and told him what happened, and Rico told him he was off the job and didn't give him another one. So your dad is out of work for right now."

Rico is my dad's boss and one of the nicest guys you'll ever meet. My dad must have really made him mad.

I grab my backpack. "I'm going to go to my room and study. Big test this week."

"And don't forget tomorrow," my mom says. "First AAU practice. Very exciting!"

"Mom," I say, "did you ever ask this coach guy how much it's going to cost? What if it's a lot? How are we going to pay for it, especially now?"

She kisses me on the top of my head. "You let me worry about that," she says. "Your job is to play ball and make me happy."

There's that word again.

Job.

AUSTIN

The first thing I realize at AAU practice is that I'm definitely the shortest person on this team.

The second thing I realize is that I don't recognize anyone else, except that kid Carter Haswell from South. But that's not surprising, since these are kids from all over the state.

And the third thing I realize is that Coach Cash is being way too nice to me.

"Guys, bring it in," Coach says, after we finish a defensive drill. We circle up. "I want to show you what I mean about bodying up on a guy. Austin, come over here a sec. Body up on me."

I do as I'm told.

"Good! Good!" Coach Cash yells. "You guys see how Austin uses his body to take up space, but keeps his hands down? That's because hands equal fouls." He smacks me on the back. "Great work, Austin."

I keep my eyes glued to the floor, which is the only way to hide my shock, since I've never heard Coach Cash say those three words together in my life.

The same kind of thing happens all practice long. Coach keeps using me to demonstrate a drill, then saying, "Great work, Austin," when I do it without messing up.

Later on, we play a scrimmage. After I do anything half-decently, guys on the team start chirping.

"Super job, Austin," says this giant dude, after I deflect a ball out of bounds.

"You're amazing, Austin," says another, after I catch a pass.

"I love you, Austin," says another kid, when I make a foul shot.

Everyone thinks it's hilarious.

As I'm running laps at the end of practice, I look up into the bleachers. There's only one person there: my dad. I hope the other guys don't know who he is, because they'll just think that's why Coach is favoring me. And they'd be right.

My dad sees me and nods. I pretend not to see him and keep running, trying to drown out the voice in my head.

You're only here because of your dad, Austin.

Right away I recognize the guy from North who told his
teammate to play hurt.

"Hey, man," I say to him at the beginning of practice.
"Austin, right?"

"Yup," he says back. "How's it going?"

"Pretty good, you?"

"Good."

We don't talk much during the rest of the workout, but I
notice how the coach is using him for every drill. It's funny at
first, but then it gets kind of annoying.

I do well in the drills. Then we start to scrimmage, and I
match up with some guy named Alonzo from upstate who's
really quick. I start a little rocky. A kid inbounds to me, and I
head upcourt. I think my handle is pretty nice, but like I said,
Alonzo is super quick, and he flicks the ball away from me for a
second, but I get it back. He's bodying up on me like Coach said,
and I slap his hand away, and he bodies up again, and I slap his
hand away again. I cross half-court and throw a pass to a kid on

the wing, but someone on the other team with super long arms steps into the passing lane and snatches it.

I can't believe it—I mess up my very first play.

The kid who stole the ball takes off down the court, and I take off after him. He angles in for the layup, I try to block it but miss the ball and crack him on top of his head. He makes the layup anyway, then glares at me.

"All day long," he sneers. Then he repeats it, slower, just in case I missed it the first time. "All. Day. Long."

I don't answer him. Instead, I think about what my dad told me—*all you have to do is be the best, every step of the way.* Up to now, that hasn't been a problem.

But all of a sudden, it might be.

I get the inbounds, take the ball up the court, and flick Alonzo's hand away. Enough of this, I think to myself. I dribble toward the wing and swing it over to the big dude underneath, then spot an opening and cut to the basket. The guy throws me a lightning-quick pass. I catch the ball in stride, weave through a couple of bodies, and head in for the layup when at the last minute I see Austin coming in from the side. I fake and Austin goes flying past me. I pull the ball back down, glide under the hoop, and flick up a reverse layup. The ball kisses high off the backboard. I don't even have to look, I know where it's going.

The swish of the net is the sweetest sound I've ever heard.

I glance up at some guy standing alone in the bleachers. He doesn't look too happy.

I run back down the floor and spot the guy who trash-talked me. He gives me a little nod of respect. I nod back.

Game on.

Man, Carter Haswell can really play basketball.

I mean, I knew he was good, but it's one thing to be good against league competition, and it's another thing to be good against the best players in the state.

After watching him rip it up during the scrimmage, I end up behind him at the water fountain.

"Man, you played great today," I tell him.

He grins. "Thanks, man. You too."

He's just being nice, but I accept his compliment with a nod.

Carter gestures over to Coach Cash. "Hey, what's the deal? You know this dude or something?"

"Yeah. He's actually my private coach."

Carter whistles. "Dang. What's that like?"

"Intense."

"In a good way?"

"Sometimes."

"Well, you must love the game, huh?"

"Sometimes."

He laughs and fills his water bottle. "Hey, how's your teammate doing? The one that got hurt?"

"He's pissed off."

"At you?"

"At everything."

We both silently decide that's enough on that topic. "Listen, man," Carter says, "I heard the guys out there, ribbing you because of the coach. Don't let them get to you. Just keep playing ball, you'll be fine."

"I appreciate that, thanks."

"All good."

We stand there for a few seconds, and it occurs to me that I could actually be friends with this guy in another life.

He picks up his gym bag and slings it over his shoulder. "Anyway, I gotta go grab the bus, see you next time. Keep up the good work."

I'm wondering what it would be like to take a bus home when my dad walks up to me. "That was Carter Haswell, right? That kid is something. Gotta figure out a way to keep him on the team."

"What do you mean?"

"Well, the program costs fifteen hundred bucks a season, and I'm pretty sure his family doesn't have two nickels to rub together. Coach Cash already got a call from his mom about it, and we're talking about putting together some sort of scholarship for him."

"Wait, why are you involved with that?"

"Because I'm one of the sponsors of the team," my dad says, as if it's the most obvious thing in the world.

"Oh, right." *Of course.*

My dad puts his sunglasses on and chuckles. "Carter smoked you out there a few times, huh? Well, now you know what it's like playing with the big boys."

I answer him by pulling out my phone and putting my ear pods in. On the ride home, I think about asking my dad to stop for ice cream, but I don't.

THURSDAY, NOVEMBER 22 11:18 AM

Star Walthorne Athlete Withdraws from School

In a week that's already seen its share of local off-the-field sports news, another bombshell dropped last night as it was revealed that Sophia Vargelle, a student at Walthorne North Middle School and a star guard on the school's basketball team, has withdrawn from school. Ms. Vargelle's family was found to have moved out of the Walthorne School District sometime last year, but the student-athlete remained enrolled at the school without special dispensation, which is in violation of state law. Sources have confirmed that Walthorne North will be forced to forfeit all games played by last season's team, which had a record of 15 wins and 5 losses and finished third in the league.

I don't know who Sophia Vargelle is. So obviously, I had no idea what she had or hadn't done until that random person called into my radio show.

But none of that matters when Janeece and Callie spot me in the lunch line.

"Hey! Alfie!"

I turn and see them walking toward me with big smiles on their faces.

"Dude!" Callie says. "Well done!"

"What do you mean?"

She smacks me on the shoulder playfully, but it hurts. "Come on! I heard what happened. Some, like, anonymous caller called in to your show and told you about that girl Sophia on Walthorne North. Then she withdraws from school! And she's, like, one of their best players! I mean come on, how awesome is that?"

"Pretty awesome, I guess," I say, just to say something.

Callie winks. "You really are some kind of investigative reporter, huh? First the kid who told the other kid to play hurt, and now this? I love it. I LOVE IT! You're taking North apart, like, one by one!"

"I actually got the Clay Elkind story wrong," I tell Callie, "and this time all I did was answer the phone."

Janeece gives me the side-eye. "What, you feel bad for that Sophia girl, because she's white, like you?"

"Of course not!" I say, shocked.

Janeece giggles. "I'm just messing with you."

"She did a bad thing, for sure," I say. "But it wasn't all her fault. I'm pretty sure her parents or coach came up with the idea."

"Doesn't matter to me, to be honest," Janeece says, shrugging. "We're gonna whup North with or without that girl. But I don't mind seeing them knocked down. They think that just because they've all got money that they can break the rules. Well, they can't."

"You know it," Callie agrees.

We get our food, and Callie bumps my tray with hers. "Come on, let's sit! We can talk about other ways to get those guys in trouble!"

I'd rather eat by myself and study for the math test, to be honest, but I'm not about to tell them that.

"Sure thing," I say.

As I walk into the cafeteria for lunch, Eddy intercepts me right away.

"Hey, what's going on?" I ask him. "Everything good?"

Eddy jerks his head behind him. "Coach Benny has lunch monitor duty, and he's looking for you. He doesn't look happy."

"Oh, great."

I keep my head down, hoping it will make me invisible, but just before we sit down, I feel a big hand—more like a paw, really—clamp down on my shoulder.

I turn to face him. "Coach Benny! What's up?"

"Hello, Mr. Haswell. Do you mind telling me what is going on with you and math?" He always likes to get straight to the point.

"I'm not sure what you mean."

"Oh, I'm sure you do." He narrows his eyes at me. "Principal Marshak came to see me this morning. Apparently she has been advised by your math instructor that you're in danger of failing math. And if you fail math, you will automatically be disqualified from participating in extracurricular activities."

We both know what that means. The only extracurricular activity I participate in is basketball.

"I understand, Coach," I say.

"Do you?" He leans into me. "I thought we talked about this. Didn't I get through to you? Nothing is more important than your schoolwork! And if you fail math, it will mean more than just missing the next game against Ackton. It will mean missing the whole season. It will mean jeopardizing your development as a player and your ability to get ready for high school ball and beyond."

"I get it, I swear." But the truth is, I don't get it. I don't get math at all, I never really tried to get it, I never asked for help, and I definitely never admitted to myself that not getting it could ruin everything.

"Are you set for this test?" Coach Benny asks.

"I hope so," I say, which isn't a lie, technically.

"Good." He scrunches up his eyebrows, which makes him look extra scary. "Because you have to figure out a way to pass this thing. Do whatever it takes. Just pass."

He finally takes his hand off my shoulder and walks away.

Eddy, Lucas, and Sham are munching away, but I'm pretty sure they heard the whole thing.

"I'm in trouble," I say. No one looks up from their food at first. Then Eddy says, "So, what are you going to do?"

I shake my head. "Pass the test, somehow."

"You been studying?" Lucas asks.

"I don't know. A little, I guess. We'll find out."

"Hold up," Sham says. "Coach told you to do whatever it takes, right?"

I nod. "Yeah. I've been trying to figure out what he meant by that."

Eddy looks confused. "What do you mean, 'what he meant by that'?"

"I mean, like, did he seriously mean whatever it takes? Because, you know, 'whatever it takes' could mean a lot of things."

"Yeah," Eddy says. "It could mean a lot of things."

I take a bite of my sandwich, with a bunch of thoughts and questions racing through my head. If I get kicked off the school team, will I get kicked off the AAU team, too? Will it really affect my development as a high school player? Will it ruin my chances at getting a college scholarship? And what will my mom do if she can't watch me play basketball?

I look back at Eddy and ask him, "Are you thinking what I'm thinking? And are you cool with it?"

"Yeah," he says, "I guess so."

"Are you sure?"

He doesn't look up from his meatball hero. "I'm sure. Now can we stop talking about it?"

And then we finish our lunches without another word.

There's a different kind of quiet in a classroom when kids are about to take a test. It's like this low hum of nervousness. People bite their nails or bounce up and down on their feet, and no one is really looking at each other. It's super tense.

And that feeling goes double when it's a math test.

As we all stumble in, our teacher, Ms. Vallone, stands in front of her desk. "Okay everyone, let's take our seats and get straight to it. The quicker we get started, the quicker this long national nightmare known as the fractions/ratios/percentages test will be over."

She's trying to be funny, but no one laughs. It's not a great time.

Ms. Vallone hands out the tests, and as I grab mine, I notice something a little strange: Carter Haswell, who is sitting two rows in front of me, slides his desk just a tiny bit closer to the kid sitting next to him, Eddy Dixon. They whisper something to each other, but I can't hear what it is.

Then Ms. Vallone says, "You may begin," and I do.

I remember the last time I was really nervous.

It was last year, third game of the season, and I got fouled with two seconds left and our team behind by one point. I had to make both free throws for us to win, and the whole gym was completely silent. I missed the first shot, but somehow managed to make the second, and we won in overtime. I can still feel my knees knocking together, and I can still see my hands shaking. It was bad.

But it wasn't half as bad as right now, as I slide my desk slightly closer to Eddy's. I'm trying to do it as softly as possible, but the scratching and scraping is loud enough to wake up dead people. At least, to me it is. But when I glance around the classroom, it doesn't look like anybody noticed a thing. Ms. Vallone hands out the tests. I glance down at mine, and I feel shame. Shame because I've never really admitted to myself that numbers are like a foreign language to me that I can't understand. Shame because I was too embarrassed to ask for help from the teacher. Shame because I didn't tell my parents about my math problems, because I convinced myself that they had too much other stuff to deal with, even though I knew that was just an excuse and the real reason was that I was just too lazy to deal with it.

But mostly, I feel shame because of what I'm about to do.

I make sure no one is looking, then I glance over to my right as Eddy turns his paper slightly in my direction, just enough so I can see it.

And then I write down the first answer.

At first, I don't think anything of it. Everyone looks around during tests. People's minds wander, or they're trying to think, or it's just something to do as they sit there and squirm their way through something they definitely don't want to be doing.

But then I see it again. Carter scans the room, then slowly turns his head to the right. His eyes drop down to Eddy's test. He leans in, just an inch or two, for a better look. Then he goes back to his own test and writes.

I watch Carter do this four times in a row. Then he doesn't do it for a while. Then, about ten minutes later, I see him do it again, three more times. I look around the room to see if anyone else saw what I saw, but it seems like no one did.

Just me.

I'm so freaked out that I almost forget to finish my test.

"Okay! Pencils down! Calculators off! We're done, people!"

As Ms. Vallone walks around to collect the tests, I keep my eyes glued to my desk. A few seconds later, I feel her hovering over me.

"Mr. Haswell, everything go okay? You never came for extra help like I asked you to."

I don't look up. "I think so. I studied a lot."

"That's good to hear." She picks up my test and moves on to Eddy. "All good, Mr. Dixon? Can I expect another A?"

"I hope so," Eddy mumbles.

"What's wrong with you boys today?" asks Ms. Vallone. "You're usually two of my loudest customers!"

I shrug. "Just tired after taking the test, Ms. V."

She smiles. "Well, I guess in its own way, math is just as much of a workout as basketball, wouldn't you say?"

I try to look at her, but the best I can do is look past her.

"That's for sure," I say.

I gather up my books, with Mr. Rashad's words ringing in my ears.

The truth is the only thing that matters.

I see Janeece, and we walk out of the classroom together. I don't want to talk about the test, so I ask about her upcoming game against Roseville.

"They played us tough last year," Janeece says, "but I think we got this. You going to broadcast the game?"

"You bet," I tell her. "Looking forward to it."

We keep talking about basketball as we walk down the hall, but I'm only paying half-attention.

The truth is the only thing that matters.

And then I think about another thing Mr. Rashad said.

Can we do anything about it?

I stop suddenly. "Oh shoot, you know something, Janeece? I think I forgot my book. You go ahead without me, I'll see you at gym."

And before she can say anything, I turn around and head back toward Ms. Vallone's room.

I can immediately feel something weird between me and Eddy.

As we walk down the hall, we don't look at each other. Sham and Lucas are making jokes, keeping things loose, but Eddy and I don't laugh. It's like some invisible wall went up and we're on opposite sides of it.

"Let's meet up before practice for some quick MasterBlaster," Sham says. He's talking about this new video game that everyone loves. "Bet we can get, like, fifteen minutes in."

"I'm down," says Lucas. "My turn to kick butt."

"Not going to happen, my friend," says Sham.

Lucas smacks him in the arm. "We'll see."

They turn to Eddy and me. "Boys? You in?"

Eddy shrugs. "I don't know. I might have some stuff I have to do."

"Before practice?" Sham asks.

My eyes flare. "He said he didn't know! Leave the guy alone."

"Whoa," Lucas says. "No need to get testy. What about you, Carter, you in?"

"I doubt it," I say. "I hate that freakin' game anyway."

Sham stops walking and stares at me. "Dude, what's up with you? You got this test behind you, you're gonna pass, Coach Benny's gonna be happy, we're gonna keep winning, it's all good."

But I don't answer him. Instead I veer off toward the bathroom.

It's all good.

Is it though?

Ms. Vallone is sitting at her desk when I walk in. I think she
might already be grading the tests we just took.

She looks up, sees me, and smiles. "Alfie, hi! Did you forget
something?"

"No, I . . . I just wanted to ask you a question."

"Sure thing, what's up?"

"Well, if, um . . . if you saw something that you knew was
wrong, but if you said something about it then someone you
know and like would get in really big trouble, what would
you do?"

"Well, I guess it depends on what they did wrong. Can you
tell me what you're referring to?"

I'm standing in front of her desk, and I suddenly feel very
alone. "I think I might have seen something."

"What kind of something?"

"Someone . . . I mean, I'm not sure . . . but I thought
maybe . . ." I stop talking, because now that I'm really doing it,
I'm suddenly filled with doubt. Maybe I actually didn't see what
I thought I saw, and after what happened with Clay, I can't make

that mistake again. Or, maybe it did really happen, but for a good reason, like Carter couldn't study because he had to take care of a sick parent or something.

Or maybe I just can't tell on another student.

"Alfie?" Ms. Vallone is staring at me.

For a second, I think about saying what happened without using any names, but then I realize that would probably just make things more confusing.

"Are you trying to tell me something, Alfie?" Ms. Vallone asks. "Are you saying someone did something wrong? With the test?"

I'm frozen, because I'm not able to say what I think I saw, but I'm not able to lie either. She must see it in my face, because her smile disappears. "I see," she says. "Well, this is a very complicated situation. I don't want to put you in a position where you jeopardize a friendship. At the same time, if you saw what I think you saw, it's a very serious matter, and you would be doing the right thing by telling me. I can assure you we would keep it totally confidential."

I realize I've been biting my nails, because I have to stop biting them to answer her. "I'm uh, I'm actually not sure, so, uh, I think maybe I shouldn't have come talk to you."

"I know you're nervous," Ms. Vallone says, in her gentlest voice. "That's understandable."

"I'm really sorry. I need to go." I turn and start to leave, just as the door to the classroom opens. I jump back like I've just seen a ghost.

But it's not a ghost.

It's Carter Haswell.

I see Alfie standing there, in front of the teacher, and I freeze.

What could they be talking about?

Ms. Vallone stands up. "Well, this is certainly a busy afternoon," she says. "Normally students run from my classroom as fast as humanly possible, but today, it seems like you kids just can't stay away." She smiles at me, but I can tell there's other stuff going on in her mind. "What can I do for you, Carter?"

"I can come back later if you're in the middle of something," I say quickly.

"Okay," Ms. Vallone says.

I start to leave, but halfway through the door, I turn back around and stop right in front of the teacher's desk.

"I did something bad," I say. I don't even care if Alfie is there to hear me. I just need to get it out, like a poison. "I did something bad today, and I'm really, really sorry."

Ms. Vallone's face deflates, like a balloon. She glances over at Alfie, who is standing there, frozen. Then Alfie's face suddenly crumbles, and she starts crying and runs out of the room. Ms.

Vallone says, "Alfie, wait!" but Alfie doesn't wait. She flies out the door and slams it behind her.

The sound echoes in the silence.

Finally, Ms. Vallone takes a deep breath and lets it out slowly. "Do you want to tell me what happened?" she asks, quietly.

But I have a question. "What was Alfie doing here?"

Ms. Vallone shakes her head. "Let's talk about what you came to see me about."

"No, seriously, why was she here?"

"I can't tell you that."

Ms. Vallone sinks slowly back into her chair, and I suddenly realize exactly what's going on.

She already knows I cheated on the test.

Because Alfie Jenks told her.

SHAM

CARTER YOU THERE?

CARTER?

DUDES I THINK HE LEFT

LUCAS

WHADDYA MEAN

SHAM

HE'S GONE

LEFT SCHOOL

EDDY

WHO TOLD YOU THAT

SHAM

AMIR SAW HIM AT HIS LOCKER GETTING HIS STUFF AND
WHEN HE ASKED CARTER WHAT WAS GOING ON HE SAID
HIS MOM WAS PICKING HIM UP

EDDY

I'M GONNA CALL HIM

LUCAS

OH MAN

SHAM

IS HE ANSWERING?

EDDY

NAH

SHAM

I'M GONNA TEXT JANEECE MAYBE SHE KNOWS WHAT'S GOING ON

EDDY

WHY WOULD SHE KNOW

SHAM

I SAW THEM TALKING IN THE HALL NEAR THE OFFICE

EDDY

CARTER CAN YOU TEXT US BACK

LUCAS

CARTER YOU GOT TO TELL US WHAT HAPPENED

SHAM

JANEECE JUST TEXTED

SAID CARTER SEEMED UPSET BUT HE WOULDN'T SAY WHY

BUT YEAH HE TOLD HER HE WAS LEAVING SCHOOL

AND WASN'T SURE WHEN HE'D BE BACK

LUCAS

OH MAN

SHAM

THIS IS BAD

EDDY

I'M FREAKING OUT RIGHT NOW YOU GUYS

FREAKING OUT

HEY IT'S ME

LUCAS

CARTER!

SHAM

DUDE!!! WHAT IS HAPPENING???

EDDY

CARTER WHAT'S GOING ON?

I COULDN'T DEAL WITH IT

I COULDN'T DEAL WITH BEING A CHEATER

I COULDN'T HANDLE IT

SO I WENT BACK INTO MS. V'S CLASS TO TELL HER WHAT I DID

BUT ALFIE JENKS WAS ALREADY THERE

SHE MUST HAVE SEEN ME COPYING EDDY'S TEST

COZ SHE WAS TALKING TO MS. V ABOUT SOMETHING AND

I WAS PRETTY SURE IT WAS ABOUT ME

COZ ALFIE LOOKED UPSET AND MS. V LOOKED LIKE SHE KNEW

SO I ENDED UP TELLING HER EVERYTHING

WHAT COACH BENNY SAID ABOUT HOW I COULDN'T PLAY IF I DIDN'T PASS

AND I TOLD HER ABOUT MY DAD LOSING HIS JOB

AND MY MOM WORKING DOUBLE SHIFTS

AND HOW I NEEDED TO BE ABLE TO PLAY BALL AND BE THE BEST

SO I COULD GET A COLLEGE SCHOLARSHIP AND ALL THAT

BUT DON'T WORRY EDDY

I TOLD HER YOU HAD NO IDEA I WAS LOOKING AT
YOUR PAPER
I SWEAR
AND MS. V LOOKED LIKE SHE WAS GOING TO CRY
AND I THOUGHT SHE WAS GOING TO BE COOL
ABOUT IT,
LIKE WE COULD FIX IT SOMEHOW
BUT SHE SAID WE HAD TO GO DOWN TO THE OFFICE
AND THEN I TOLD PRINCIPAL MARSHAK
AND SHE SAID THEY WOULD NEED SOME TIME TO
FIGURE IT OUT,
BUT THAT IN THE MEANTIME I HAD TO GO HOME
AND I WOULD PROBABLY BE SUSPENDED
FROM SCHOOL
AND FROM THE TEAM TOO
AND MY MOM HAD TO LEAVE WORK TO PICK ME UP
SHE WAS CRYING

SHAM

NOOOOOOOOOOOOOOOOO
DUDE I AM SSSSOOOO SORRY

LUCAS

HUGS MAN

EDDY

I'M REALLY REALLY SORRY CARTER

ALSO WOW, OUR TEAM IS GOING TO SUCK BIG TIME NOW

NAH

YOU GUYS WILL BE OK

IT IS WHAT IT IS

MY FAULT

I'LL GET THROUGH IT

I MEAN, IT SUCKS

BUT YOU KNOW WHAT

I FEEL BETTER ANYWAY

LUCAS

I'LL TELL YOU WHAT, THAT GIRL ALFIE IS GONNA HAVE
SOME PROBLEMS

MS. V WOULDN'T TELL ME WHAT THEY WERE

TALKING ABOUT,

BUT I MEAN, COME ON,

WHAT ELSE WAS ALFIE DOING THERE,

AND THEN SHE FREAKS OUT AND

RUNS OUT OF THE ROOM WHEN I GET THERE

SHAM

OH YOU KNOW IT, SHE'S LIKE SUCH A LOSER

WORSE

A SNITCH

EDDY

SERIOUSLY

WHAT IS WRONG WITH HER

LUCAS

NOT COOL

WHATEVER

I DON'T EVEN CARE

I'LL LET YOU GUYS KNOW WHEN I KNOW WHAT'S

GOING ON

EDDY

HANG IN THERE

LUCAS

STAY CHILL MAN

SHAM

BE COOL

CARTER?

CARTER?

HEY I JUST WANT YOU TO KNOW I DIDN'T SAY ANYTHING

I SWEAR

ARE YOU THERE?

I MEAN I DID SEE WHAT YOU WERE DOING
BUT I WASN'T SURE WHAT I SAW AND
I WAS TRYING TO FIGURE IT OUT WHEN I WAS TALKING
TO MS. V
BUT I HAD TOTALLY DECIDED I WASN'T GOING TO
SAY ANYTHING
I WAS CONFUSED
YOU CAN ASK MS V

CARTER ARE YOU THERE? PLS ANSWER ME

I'M REALLY SORRY ABOUT EVERYTHING

WHY ARE YOU SORRY IF YOU DIDN'T TELL HER?

I DIDN'T MEAN IT LIKE THAT!
I MEANT I'M SORRY FOR WHAT YOU'RE GOING THROUGH!!!

IT'S MY FAULT
I DID IT
DON'T WORRY ABOUT IT
IT'S NOT YOUR FAULT
JUST LEAVE ME ALONE.

FRIDAY, NOVEMBER 23 7:17 PM

Legendary Coach Steps Down After Possible Infraction

In a surprising development that stunned the local sports world, Benjamin Walters stepped down today from his position as head basketball coach and director of the physical education department at Walthorne South Middle School.

Mr. Walters, who was elected to the state athletic Hall of Fame after coaching the Walthorne High School basketball team to six state titles in a legendary twenty-two-year career, had come out of retirement four years ago to help Walthorne South revive its basketball program after budget cuts had previously forced its elimination. He led the team to two league championships without incident until earlier this week, when reports surfaced that Coach Walters had urged one of his best players to cheat on a test, to ensure that he would pass the class and be able to stay on the team.

Coach Walters released the following statement this morning, through the office of the Walthorne Board of Education:

"In the last several days, misinformation has been spread online that I encouraged a student at Walthorne South Middle School to overcome a failing grade through improper means. This is absolutely not true, I would never do such a thing, but I confess that I may not have been as judicious in my words as I should have been, and it appears that the student misinterpreted my intentions. I regret this action, but it should in no way reflect poorly on this particular student, or any student at Walthorne South, who are all battling budget cuts, financial struggles, and other obstacles as they strive to get an education and better themselves. Therefore, to avoid being a further distraction, I have decided to step down as Head Basketball Coach and Director of Physical Education, effective immediately. I will have no further comment on this matter."

There have been reports that the student in question was suspended from school as well as the team, but school officials refused to confirm this.

As of this writing, the school has not named a successor to Mr. Walters.

PROWLING WITH THE PANTHERS
A SPORTS BLOG BY ALFIE JENKS
SATURDAY, NOVEMBER 24

Hi again everyone, it's Alfie, back to talk (well actually write about) sports.

Usually, I write about how the local school teams are doing, because that's what I always thought sports reporting was: giving the scores and describing what happened. But now, I'm realizing that there is more to it than just what happens on the court, or on the field. And today, I want to focus on another topic.

And that topic is: Have we gotten too serious about sports?

This is hard for me to say because I love sports so much. No one is more intense about sports than me! I've never been very good at playing them, but they are definitely the most important part of my life, except for my family, of course. And I have so much respect for everyone who plays, or coaches, or referees or umpires, or works in sports in any way. Especially sports for kids, because a lot of people are volunteering their time.

But I've noticed that when it comes to youth sports, sometimes people forget that these are just kids playing a game. Whether it's parents screaming at the referee, or coaches screaming at the players, or even kids screaming at each other, sometimes the last thing you think about when you're watching sports these days is that it's supposed to be FUN.

I was reminded of that this week when it was announced that the legendary Coach Walters resigned from Walthorne South Middle School after rumors surfaced that he encouraged a star basketball player to cheat so he could pass a class and stay on the team. I do not know if the coach actually did that or not, and if there is one thing I've learned, it's to make sure to report only the facts and to not jump to conclusions. But I think we can all agree that just the fact that it's even possible—that a coach may have told a player to cheat—shows that the pressure on thirteen- and fourteen-year-olds playing sports has gone too far. Last week, it was discovered that an athlete was still enrolled at Walthorne North just so she could play on the basketball team, even though she had moved out of the district months ago. And earlier this season, a star athlete on Walthorne North's basketball team was badly injured after he was allowed to play hurt.

If you ask me, these are all examples of youth sports spinning out of control. I think we all need to look in the mirror—myself included—and ask ourselves why kids' lives are being turned upside down for something that's supposed to be done for enjoyment and exercise!

I love sports, and I always will. But just because we love something doesn't mean it's perfect. I love my parents, too, and they're DEFINITELY not perfect.

Sorry Mom and Dad!

WALTHORNESPIRIT.COM

Sunday at 7:20 pm

Chase Hey yo, who is this Alfie Jenks person

Like · Reply

Sunday at 7:23 pm

Lucas Why

Like · Reply

Sunday at 7:27 pm

Chase I heard he ratted out your best player and got him kicked off the team
That's freakin hilarious

Like · Reply

Sunday at 7:29 pm

Amir First of all Alfie is a girl
And second of all what do you care
Aren't you the kid who doesn't even go to North

Like · Reply

Sunday at 7:32 pm

Chase Whatever
I still think it's awesome

Like · Reply

Sunday at 7:35 pm

Alfie That's not what happened

Like · Reply

Sunday at 7:38 pm

Kevin This kid Alfie is like a one-man wrecking crew
Even if she is a girl ☺

Like · Reply

Sunday at 7:39 pm

Clementine What is that supposed to mean

Like · Reply

Sunday at 7:42 pm

Kevin I mean come on

First she accuses our coach of making Clay play hurt, and so Austin ends up taking the blame, and then the thing happens with Sophia Vargelle. We thought this Alfie kid was just going after North kids, but nope, now she gets YOUR best guy kicked off the team and your famous coach resigns in disgrace, I mean c'mon that's WILD right??

Like · Reply

Sunday at 7:44 pm

Sham You don't know what you're talking about

We are dealing with it over here

just stay out of it

Like · Reply

Sunday at 7:47 pm

Ashley Sophia is my best friend and she was so devastated

It wasn't her idea, she was just doing what people told her to do

And now everyone thinks she's just a cheat

You guys at south should be ashamed of yourselves

I'm glad it came out that you're cheaters too

Like · Reply

Sunday at 7:51 pm

Sham You all really need to stop yapping right now

Carter is THE MAN and he owned up to his mistake right away

Like · Reply

Sunday at 7:54 pm

North4Eva Yeah after he got caught

Like · Reply

Sunday at 7:59 pm

Austin This is just not cool

Everyone needs to chill out

Carter was cool with me after the Clay thing

I hope he's doing alright

Like · Reply

Sunday at 8:03 pm

Chase Austin, why you got to be so nice all the time?

You need to man up a little

I'm sure your dad would agree

Like · Reply

Sunday at 8:05 pm

Austin Shut up Chase

Like · Reply

Sunday at 8:07 pm

Chase Ouchie

Like · Reply

Sunday at 8:14 pm

North4Eva I guess the one thing we can all agree on is that this girl Alfie is a problem

Like · Reply

Sunday at 8:17 pm

Eddy Don't worry about it

Like · Reply

Sunday at 8:22 pm

North4Eva Oh and good luck trying to win any more games this season

Like · Reply

Sunday at 8:23 pm

Eddy We'll win more than you I can promise you that

Like · Reply

Sunday at 8:27 pm

Kevin I don't care as long as we crush you last game of the season

Like · Reply

Sunday at 8:29 pm

Amir We'll see about that

Like · Reply

Sunday at 8:32 pm

Chase Just try not to get arrested before then

Like · Reply

Sunday at 8:37 pm

Sham I can't wait to see you guys on the court again.
I. CANNOT. WAIT.

Like · Reply

YO CARTER

IT'S AUSTIN CHAMBERS

JUST WANTED TO SAY SORRY MAN AND EVERYONE
MAKES MISTAKES

I KNOW I DO

THANKS MAN I APPRECIATE THAT

YOU'RE A GOOD DUDE

I REMEMBER AFTER THE CLAY THING YOU TOLD ME NOT
TO BLAME MYSELF

YOU DIDN'T HAVE TO DO THAT

WELL YOU DIDN'T HAVE TO TEXT ME TODAY

SO WE'RE EVEN

BUT SERIOUSLY

THX

I'LL BE OK

GOT MY GUITAR

YOU PLAY GUITAR, THAT'S COOL

BARELY ☺

HAHA, WELL HANG IN THERE

FOR SURE. DON'T LET THE AAU GUYS RIP YOU TOO
BAD EITHER

YEAH I'LL TRY NOT TO.
I'LL SEE YOU BACK OUT ON THE COURT SOON

HOPEFULLY SOON MAN
WE'LL SEE.

SECOND HALF

WWMS

WALTHORNE SOUTH RADIO

ALFIE: Hello and welcome to Talking Sports
                on this December 3rd, my name is
                Alfie Jenks. The big news this week
                continues to be the Walthorne South
                boys basketball team, which is still
                trying to recover from the suspension
                of star guard Carter Haswell and the
                resignation of Coach Benny Walters.
                After losing two games in a row under
                new coach Leonard Rickson, they got
                back on the winning track last night
                against Simonton, as Lucas Burdeen
                led the way with 12 points. I tried
                to get Lucas on today's show to
                talk about his excellent game, but
                unfortunately he wasn't available
                for comment . . .

                          **

                This is Talking Sports, my name is
                Alfie Jenks. In this last week before
                the holiday break, the Walthorne South
                girls basketball team, led by Janeece
                Renfro, continues to dominate the
                league, winning their sixth straight
                game last night, 44–29. Janeece got

her third double-double of the season,
collecting 19 points and 10 rebounds.
Meanwhile, on the boys side, both
local middle schools continue to
struggle. The traditional powerhouses
are each without their best players,
with Carter Haswell of South out on
suspension and Clay Elkind of North
still recovering from a bad leg injury
he suffered in the opening game
against South. Leading scorers Lucas
Burdeen for South and Austin Chambers
for North have done their best to
pick up the slack, but as of now,
both teams are in danger of missing
the playoffs . . .

**

Hello and welcome to Talking Sports,
my name is Alfie Jenks. Well, it's the
middle of January, and for the first
time since the program was revived
four years ago, the Walthorne South
Middle School boys basketball team
has fallen below .500, as a loss to
Canton last night lowered their record
to 5 wins and 6 losses. Amir Watkins
led the team with 11 points and Eddy
Dixon had 2 steals.

No players were available for comment.

**

Hello and welcome to Talking Sports,
my name is Alfie Jenks. It's the last
week in February, and the basketball
playoffs are right around the corner.
But with a chance to secure the last
playoff spot, the Walthorne South
boys basketball team fell last night
to Marenham Central, 42–36. That
brings their record to 9 wins and 10
losses. They have one game to go in
the season, and it is the traditional
Friday night season-ending game
against Walthorne North, which also
has a record of 9 and 10. As it turns
out, whoever wins that game will get
the last spot in the league playoffs.
Meanwhile, the girls team continues
to roll, defeating Monmouth 50 to 35.
They bring their 16 and 3 record into
their last game, which is also against
Walthorne North, on Thursday night,
the night before the boys game. Should
be quite a week for basketball fans!

I've broadcast fourteen basketball games over the last three months, both girls and boys.

I've done sports reports every Tuesday and Thursday.

I think I'm getting better at it.

Mr. Rashad says I have real talent and that I should never apologize for pursuing the truth. Last week, he told me that he's already talked to the media advisor at the high school about me.

My parents listen to all my games, and all of my shows, and tell me that they're really proud of me.

I wrote to Doris Burke, the amazing ESPN basketball announcer, and she wrote me back, telling me to keep up the good work.

But none of that makes me feel any better when I eat lunch alone.

Today, though, I'm halfway through my slice of pizza when Janeece and Callie come over to my table and sit down.

I try to make a joke. "What are you guys doing? Don't you know there's a law against sitting here?"

They both laugh awkwardly. Then Janeece puts a clipboard

down in front of me. "So, uh, we were wondering if you would sign this."

"What is it?"

"It's a petition to get Carter reinstated to the basketball team for the last game."

I thumb through the pages. It looks like the entire school has signed. "Wow. This is pretty impressive. Looks like you got everybody."

Callie clears her throat nervously. "Yeah, pretty much, but we figured, you know, if the girl who actually told on him signed it, that would be meaningful to, like, the principal and whoever else has to decide."

"I didn't tell on him. You can ask Ms. Vallone," I say. I feel like I've said that sentence about fifty times over the last three months. But no one is listening.

"It doesn't matter," Janeece says, even though it does matter, a lot. "I don't even care. I'm not mad at you, anyway. Carter Haswell is the one who cheated. It was his fault and he knows it."

"If it's Carter's fault, then how come I'm the one eating lunch by myself every day?"

Janeece and Callie look at each other, then back at me. "Are you going to sign it or not?" Callie asks.

I sign it.

"Thanks, Alfie," Janeece says. "And no matter what happened, I still think you're, like, an amazing sports announcer."

"Thank you."

"You're welcome."

They get up from the table and start to walk away.

"Yes, by the way," I say to Janeece.

She turns back, confused. "Huh?"

"To answer your question from three months ago, yes, I think Carter has a crush on you."

Her face breaks into a giant grin before she can control it. "Oh, wow! Uh, huh, well, whatever, who cares, right?"

You do, I want to tell her, but I don't.

"Hey Alfie, you want to come sit with us?" Callie says. "I mean, everyone makes mistakes, right? I think people are over it by now."

"Thanks," I tell her. "I'll be over in a minute."

"Cool!"

They walk away.

I finish my lunch alone and then leave.

I was suspended from school for three days and suspended from the basketball team until, according to the letter my mom got, "Carter has shown marked improvement in both academic performance and personal judgment."

The AAU program said they will take me back only if I'm reinstated to the school team.

Coach Benny lost his job because of me.

Or maybe I got suspended because of him?

I'm honestly not sure.

My friends try to make me laugh, and sometimes it works, but usually it doesn't. Most people at school have been really nice, even the teachers, but one day a few weeks ago Sham and I were walking down the hall, and another kid on the basketball team, a skinny seventh grader named Paul Mastrano, ran up to me and said, "Hey Carter, so, yeah, uh, I just wanted to say that just because you're a big basketball star, everyone thinks you're, like, the victim here. But you're not. You cheated and because of you, our team is doing really badly, and also, I don't get to get coached by the guy who is, like, a total legend and the greatest coach ever. And my parents are really mad about that, and so are some other parents and kids, even if they don't tell you. So, yeah, I just thought you ought to know that."

"Dude, are you serious right now?" Sham barked. Paul was just standing there, breathing hard, with his body tense, like he half-expected me to hit him or something.

But I wasn't mad. The kid was right, and pretty brave, too. "Yeah, man, I agree," I told him. "See you around."

Paul looked shocked. "See you around too," he said, and then took off down the hall.

I've been practicing a lot of basketball, like every day for hours. I watch the team's games from the last row of the bleachers, where no one can see me. The guys are hanging in there. It hurts to watch.

Guitar is going pretty well. I taught myself "Purple Rain" the other day. I'm getting okay at chords, but I will *never* allow anyone to hear me attempt a solo.

Eddy has been tutoring me in math, and I've been paying attention this time. I got a 71 on the last test. The right way.

My dad is still looking for a job. Rico said he's trying to find a project for him, but nothing has come through so far.

My mom is still working double shifts at the assisted living center, so I barely see her. She still smiles when she sees me, and hugs and kisses me, and says she loves me, but I know I broke her heart a little. The only thing she ever said to me about it was, "You made a mistake. Learn from it. And never do it again."

I haven't spoken to Alfie Jenks since the day it happened.

AUSTIN

Turns out that my dad was right—Clay Elkind getting injured was really good for my game.

Without Clay in the lineup, I've had to pick up the slack offensively, and I've been shooting the ball well. I scored 21 points against Ackerton, which is my all-time high, and at the steakhouse after the game, my dad forgot to tell me everything I did wrong. He wanted to go over every basket, and the ice cream sundae was delicious.

He didn't seem to care that we'd lost, 51–43.

On AAU, Coach Cash has been starting me at the point, which basically means my job is to dish to KJ, our massive center, or Darian, our two-guard who barely ever misses from three. I think pretty much everyone on the team knows that this kid named Alonzo should be starting ahead of me, since he's the best ball handler I've ever seen and a lightning-quick passer, but no one says anything, because I think word is out by now that my parents are one of the main sponsors of the team. Coach Cash even lets my sister, Liv, sit on the bench at the end of games, if we're winning by a lot. And we usually are. This team is really good, even without Carter.

We're 9 and 3 after we beat Runs'n'Guns, a program from upstate. In the postgame circle, Coach Cash makes an announcement. "Guys, we've got our first overnight tournament coming up in a few weeks, the Mid-Atlantic Invitational. We're going to be playing teams from the tristate area—some terrific competition. I know some of their coaches, these are some really good clubs. We're going to be sending out an email with hotel information and costs, but I've got some great news to get us started; we'll be traveling in style, courtesy of a luxury coach bus provided by the Chambers family. Three cheers for that!"

Yells and whistles echo through the gym, and guys start high-fiving each other, but when I go to fist-bump KJ, he mumbles "Nah, I'm good," and turns away.

Darian sees the whole thing. "Don't worry about him," he tells me. "He's good buds with Alonzo, and, you know, that puts him in kind of a tough spot."

"Yeah, I get it."

As the rest of my teammates chatter excitedly about the upcoming tournament, I realize that even though everyone's totally fired up about the idea of a luxury bus, it just makes me look even more like the spoiled rich kid who's only on the team because of his rich parents.

I wish they were wrong.

> HEY EVERYONE
> JUST BACK FROM THE DOC AND I FINALLY
> HEARD THE WORDS I'VE BEEN WAITING
> TO HEAR FOR THREE MONTHS
> YOU ARE CLEARED TO PLAY
> ☺
> JUST IN TIME FOR THE GAME AGAINST SOUTH
> LET'S DO THIS

YO, CLAY, THAT'S AWESOME NEWS!! ☺

YEAH, I KNOW, PRETTY COOL RIGHT?
ALMOST CAN'T BELIEVE IT

SO THE DOC SAID YOU CAN START PRACTICING RIGHT AWAY?

PRETTY MUCH.
I'VE BEEN WORKING OUT ON MY OWN A LOT
BUT SHE SAID I CAN PRACTICE WITH THE TEAM
AND I'M GOOD TO PLAY AGAINST SOUTH

THAT'S SO AWESOME

YEAH

WE WIN WE'RE IN THE PLAYOFFS

I KNOW

IT WILL BE GREAT TO HAVE YOU OUT THERE.

YUP

HEY ARE YOU DOING ANYTHING RIGHT NOW?

NOT MUCH WHY

WANT TO MEET ME AT TOMPKINS PARK?
MAYBE SHOOT AROUND A LITTLE BIT?

I DON'T KNOW MAN, I GOT HOMEWORK

JUST FOR A LITTLE WHILE
I WANT TO SEE YOU WITH A BASKETBALL IN YOUR HANDS.
MAN I DIDN'T EVEN KNOW YOU WERE PRACTICING ON
YOUR OWN

I DIDN'T WANT TO SAY ANYTHING IN CASE I DIDN'T
MAKE IT BACK
JUST BEEN WORKING ON SOME THINGS

AWESOME.
SO YOU IN?
MEET THERE IN 30?

YEAH SURE I GUESS SO

COOL!!
SEE YOU THERE

AUSTIN

My dad used to take me down to the Tompkins Park courts when I could barely walk. They have a seven-foot hoop that I used to shoot at, and by the time I was eleven I could dunk on it.

I'm pretty sure that was the last time I ever felt tall on a basketball court.

It's a cold day, so no one is around when I get to the courts to meet Clay. I start shooting threes at the short hoop.

Swish. Swish. Miss. Swish. Swish.

My shooting percentage is high on that basket.

I start dunking.

My percentage goes up even higher when I dunk.

I start daydreaming about being six-five and dunking on a ten-foot basket. I think about the Bryce Jordan Center, the awesome, fifteen-thousand-seat arena at Penn State where my dad takes me when he goes back for reunions and stuff. I think about what it would be like to play on that court. *Chambers slides between two defenders and goes up for the Tomahawk Jam . . . And the Nittany Lions win the NCAA championship! Listen to that crowd—*

"Who you talking to?"

I turn around and Clay is standing there, smiling. It feels like a long time since I've seen him smile—at me, anyway. He's been around the team all season, on crutches at first, then in that giant ski-boot thing, but he hasn't been doing a lot of laughing. And he and I never really figured out how to get things back to the way they were before he got hurt.

But now seems like a good time to try.

"I guess I'm just talking to myself," I tell him. "In my head, I've been playing for Penn State since I was about five years old."

"And let me guess—you guys always win."

"Pretty much."

Clay holds his hands up in the universal sign for *Pass me the ball*. I zip it over to him, and he jams it in the short hoop without even jumping. I try to imagine how it must feel to be able to do that, but I can't. I feel a jolt of jealousy pass through my body, as I realize my days as the best player on Walthorne North—or any team, ever—are probably over. I tell myself to not think that way, but watching Clay make a few moves and do a few reverse jams, I realize it's not going to be easy.

"Yo, you look totally ready to go," I say.

"Yep, I'm good."

"Just in time, too."

Clay tosses the ball back to me. "Let's go play on the big boy hoops," he says. "A little one-on-one?"

"Totally."

We start playing, and sure enough, it's clear that Clay is still way better than me. He's a little rusty at first, but before long he's got it all working: the inside moves, the soft touch on the jumper, the quick hands on defense. For a few minutes, the resentment lingers, as I admit to myself once and for all that I'll never be the player he is.

But then, as we keep playing, the most amazing thing happens.

It stops bothering me.

The jolt of jealousy is gone. On this court, just the two of us playing one-on-one, I stop thinking about all the stuff I usually think about, like why I'm not as tall as Clay, or as talented as him, or as talented as my dad, or even my little sister.

I'm just outside in the park, playing ball, having a blast.

We play to twenty-one. I play Clay pretty tight, and when I hit a three (which counts for two points in one-on-one), I close the gap to 18–14. But after Clay blocks my next shot, he hits a three, then backs me down to the hoop and finishes me off with a sweet baby hook.

We slap hands.

"Nice game," Clay says. He's bent over, his hands on his knees, and he's breathing hard.

"Well, if nothing else, I made you work for it," I tell him.

He laughs. "Got to get in game shape. If only for one game."

We go to the sideline and take long swigs from our water bottles. Then Clay says, "Remember when we used to come here? Like, four, five years ago?"

"Sure, yeah. Why?"

"I don't know, I just thought of it for some reason." He points at a bike rack near the restroom area. "We used to park our bikes right over there. And we'd play pickup games for hours. It was so fun, especially that one summer. Remember?"

"Yeah, of course I remember. That was awesome."

"Yeah."

We sit quietly for a few minutes.

I wonder if he's thinking about what I'm thinking about.

How different things were back then.

No parents, no coaches, no leagues.

Just ball.

SUMMER
Four years ago

It's one of those hot, humid summer days that's too brutal for everyone except a bunch of kids who just want to play hoops in the park.

The courts are crowded, like always. Some kids know each other, some don't, but everyone is there for the same reason.

To play basketball.

The old church bell on the corner strikes once, and everyone knows what that means. The adults and older players have to clear the court, and the elementary school kids have it to themselves. It's called Free Shoot, it's every Saturday from 1 to 3, and for a lot of them it's the best two hours of the week.

Free Shoot always starts with twenty minutes of crazy running around, shooting at both baskets, mostly boys, a few girls, everyone crashing into each other, that kind of thing. Two adults are in charge of managing the courts, but as long as no one is bullying and no one gets hurt, they don't get involved.

Finally, a boy who's no more than three feet tall holds his hand up. "Yo! We need to choose sides. Who wants to be captains?"

All the kids seem to step back and make a circle around two kids in the middle.

It's unspoken, but everyone agrees that they're the two best players.

One boy has intense blue eyes and wears a throwback Allen Iverson jersey. The other boy is a little shorter, with shaggy blond hair and glasses that he keeps pushing up the bridge of his nose.

The two boys nod at each other. "You should get those sports goggles they have," the boy in the Iverson jersey tells the other boy.

"Yeah, maybe," says the boy with the glasses.

The captains pick teams. At first they pick their friends. But then the boy in the Iverson Jersey points at an extremely tall boy he's never seen before. "K, I'll take you."

The extremely tall boy glances at the boy with the glasses, who's his friend. The boy with the glasses nods. The tall boy goes to stand next to his new teammates. He doesn't know any of them.

From that point on, each captain picks some friends, some strangers. There are seven boys and one girl on one team, six boys and two girls on the other.

The game begins. The teams are even. Substitutions are made when the players on the sidelines just run onto the court and tell another player to take a break. Fouls are called by the person who commits the foul, not by the person who is fouled. There's the nine- and ten-year-old version of trash talking. There's laughter. There's competition.

At one point there is a dispute, when the ball goes out of bounds and no one can agree on who touched it last. "It's off you!" shouts a boy on one team. "No, it's off you!" shouts a girl on the other team. Everyone argues for a minute or so, until the boy with the glasses steps up and says, "I have an idea. Let's just do rock paper scissors to decide. One takes it."

Everyone agrees that this is a very good idea. The boy shoots it out with the girl. The boy takes paper, the girl takes scissors. The girl wins. Her team gets the ball. Argument over.

After that, everyone agrees—whenever there is a dispute about a foul, or who touched the ball last when it goes out of bounds, the players will resolve it the same way: rock paper scissors. One takes it.

They end up playing four games. The teams are switched around several times.

Finally, after two hours, one of the adults blows a whistle.

Free Shoot is over.

The kids are exhausted and dripping with sweat, but they're joking around.

By now, they're all friends.

As the kid with the Allen Iverson shirt and the kid with the glasses walk off the court side by side, they realize two things: one, that they never played on the same team, because they were the captains; and two, they never learned each other's names.

The blond kid with the glasses sticks out his hand. "Hey," he says. "I'm Carter."

The kid in the Allen Iverson shirt squints, his eyes shining in the afternoon sun. "Nice to meet you," he says. "I'm Austin."

They nod at each other.

"See you next week."

They play basketball with each other for the next seven Saturdays.

Then summer ends, and they don't see each other again for a long time.

It hits me, all of a sudden—Carter Haswell was the other captain.

The kid with the glasses.

"Hey," I say to Clay, as we sit there. "Is that kid Haswell still suspended from the team?"

"I don't know," he says. "I hope so. We'll beat them easy if he is."

I shake my head. "I hope he plays. Both teams should have their best players. And we have ours."

It takes Clay a second to realize I'm talking about him.

"You're right," he says, "I hope he does play." After a second, he adds, "And thanks."

It's amazing how, sometimes, just a day playing ball in the park can make everything cool.

CARTER

I'm walking down the hall at school, trying not to look at all the pep rally posters on the walls for the upcoming game against Walthorne North, when Principal Marshak stops me.

"Mr. Haswell. Nice to see you."

"It's nice to see you, too," I say back, even though it's never nice to see the principal.

She looks serious, but her eyes are soft, not hard. "I'm sure you know that a petition has been circulating, asking for your reinstatement to the basketball team."

"I do know that."

"I've been impressed with the student body for taking this initiative."

I'm not exactly sure what she's getting at, but it sounds promising and I don't want to jinx it by saying the wrong thing, so I just say, "Me too."

"I know this has been a difficult time for you," Principal Marshak says. "I know you miss doing what you love. I would like your parents to come in tomorrow to talk with me and

Coach Rickson about the situation, and perhaps we can put this incident behind us once and for all."

I can feel my heart beating. "Are you . . . are you saying I might be able to play?"

She puts her hand gently on my shoulder. "I'm saying, let's have a conversation and see what happens."

So that's how I end up sitting outside Principal Marshak's office, in between my parents. My mom is looking at her watch because she had to ask for an early lunch hour. My dad is wearing the only tie he owns, and he keeps pulling at it. What I think he really wants to do is yank it off and throw it in the trash.

I realize that parents are just as uncomfortable in the principal's office as kids are.

Finally, Principal Marshak sticks her head out of her office. "Carter? Mr. and Ms. Haswell?"

My mom smiles and says, "I actually go by my maiden name now. It's Raines."

"I see, my apologies. Why don't you all come on in?"

We file in quietly. Coach Rickson is sitting there, and so is Mr. Rashad, the guidance counselor guy, and my math teacher, Ms. Vallone. Everyone introduces themselves, and then

Principal Marshak says, "Mr. Haswell, Ms. Raines, I wanted you to come here today so we could discuss Carter's situation. As you will recall, we all met after the incident in math class, and it was decided at that time to suspend Carter from the basketball team indefinitely. His infraction was very serious, the most serious a student can commit. But now, as the season is drawing to a close, and after having follow-up conversations with both Ms. Vallone and Mr. Rashad, I thought it might be a good time to revisit that decision."

My mom raises her hand, like she's back in class. "May I say something?"

"Of course," says the principal.

"Thank you." My mom clears her throat nervously. "I think Carter has definitely learned his lesson."

Mr. Rashad leans forward. "Can you explain what you mean?"

My mom hesitates, so my dad jumps in. "I can help with that. We're not a rich family, as I'm sure you know, and I lost my job not too long ago, so I've been out of work. And well, I think somewhere along the way, Carter got the idea that he needed to use his god-given ability at basketball to help the family, by getting special treatment, and maybe one day getting a scholarship to play in college and making it all the way to the pros. So, that's why he was so desperate to pass math. So he could stay on the team."

Mr. Rashad clears his throat softly. "Do you know how difficult the odds are, in terms of getting a college scholarship, much less making it to the pros?"

"Yes, of course we do," my mom answers. "That doesn't mean it's not worth trying. Coach Benny thinks he has the talent. He told me himself."

Principal Marshak takes her glasses off and looks at me. "I think it might be time to hear from Carter about all this."

I sit up a bit straighter. "I . . . I guess it's true that I started thinking this year that basketball was more than just something to do for fun. I mean, I realized I was good—I guess really good, some people said—and that it might be a way to get someplace in life. My mom didn't, like, pressure me or anything, but I knew how much it meant to her. And Coach Benny, I mean, I feel so bad about what happened to him, but when he said that thing about doing whatever it took to pass the test, and thinking about how if I didn't, then basketball would be taken away from me, and how it would mess everything up, I just . . . I just panicked. And as soon as I did it, I felt horrible and I came back into the room to tell Ms. Vallone everything, but Alfie Jenks was already there and I was too late. And I said it before but I'm really, really sorry."

Ms. Vallone leans forward in her chair. "Carter, I thought you knew this. Alfie never told me what happened. She did see what you had done, and she was upset about it, but she was confused, and a little scared, and I don't think she wanted you to get in trouble. So she didn't say anything. You need to believe me on this."

I stare at her. "Really?"

She smiles, but it's a sad smile. "Really."

I feel something leave my body.

Maybe it's anger.

"Oh, wow," I say.

Mr. Rashad says, "Carter, you have learned some valuable lessons here, which is the most important thing going forward. And I want you, and your parents, to know that I am always available to discuss any of these kinds of issues, should they arise in the future."

"Well!" says Principal Marshak, putting her glasses back on. "There is some good to come out of this situation. Carter, you've spoken eloquently and remorsefully here today, and Ms. Vallone has informed me that you have improved your math grade significantly. You have one game left in your middle school career, and I would like for you to be able to participate. Therefore, I am pleased to tell you that you may rejoin the basketball team, effective immediately."

I had a feeling this might happen, but now that it has, I'm not sure I believe it. "Wait, what? Immediately, like, right now? I can practice with the team, and I can play against North?"

The Principal smiles. "You can, but more to the point, you may."

"Thank you. That is . . . that is so awesome." I'm not sure what else to say, so I just say again, "Thank you. Thank you so much!"

Principal Marshak puts her hand on my shoulder.

"Go out there Friday night," she says, "and make your parents proud."

AUSTIN

Either my mom or dad always drops me off at AAU practice fifteen minutes early, so I can get some extra shooting in.

Not my choice.

I'm working on my three from the corner as teammates come trickling in. With Darian, Philip, and KJ, I do that thing where we nod but don't really look at each other. When Alonzo walks in, he walks right by me.

And then I see Carter Haswell walk in.

The other guys stop shooting and run over to him. Hugs, high fives, excited chatter. Part of it is because they're happy to see him, since he hasn't been to practice in a few months. The other part is that they really like the guy, he's a great basketball player, and his dad didn't sponsor the team just so his son could be on it.

I walk over to join the reunion. Most of the guys ignore me, but Carter sticks out his hand. "How's it going?"

"Welcome back," I say. "If you're here, then that must mean you're back on the school team, too."

He grins. "Yup. Just in time to whomp you guys on Friday."

"Ha, we'll see."

He starts lacing up his sneakers, and I sit down next to him. "By the way," I say. "I realized something. We used to play against each other at the Tompkins Park courts that one summer, you remember?"

"You mean like, four, five years ago? Free Shoot?"

"Yep."

"Oh man, yeah, I totally remember! You were tall then!"

"I guess so."

"Sorry dude, I didn't mean it like that."

"It's all good. What happened to those glasses you used to wear?"

Carter laughs. "Oh man, those were nasty! When my mom got insurance at her job, I was finally able to get contacts."

"Cool." I start spinning the ball on my finger. "Good to have you back."

"Good to be back. See you out there."

We're a good team without Carter, but we're a different team with him. There's something about the way he sees the court, and how he knows things are going to happen before they actually happen, that all the "AGAIN!"s in the world can't teach you.

The kid just has that thing.

We're running a scrimmage, and I'm bringing the ball upcourt, with Alonzo draped all over me. I look over at Coach Cash, who signals a play in from the sideline: a pick-and-roll on the left elbow. KJ, who's being guarded by Carter, comes out to set the pick. Alonzo gets blocked by the pick, but Carter decides to stay on KJ instead of coming out to get me, because KJ is the bigger offensive threat. I see a lane to the hoop open up, and I decide to take it. Alonzo is really fast, though, and as I go up for the short jumper he swats the ball out of my hands and out of bounds.

TWEEEEET!

Coach Cash blows his whistle. "Foul! Alonzo, I've told you this before, but you can't put your hands on him from behind. That'll get called every time."

Alonzo waves his hand in disgust. "That is bull, man, I didn't even touch him," he mumbles to himself.

But Coach Cash has long ears. "Sorry? What was that, Alonzo?"

Alonzo shuffles his feet uncomfortably. "I didn't say anything."

"I thought I heard you say that was bull."

"Nah, man. You heard wrong."

Uh-oh. The rest of us glance at each other. You're not supposed to talk to the coach like that.

Coach Cash's ears get red. "Excuse me? EXCUSE ME?" He gets up in Alonzo's face. "Get off my court! NOW!"

As Alonzo shuffles slowly off the court, Coach Cash blows his whistle. "Tyson!" he yells to one of the kids on the sidelines. "Get in here for Alonzo!" Coach throws me the ball. "Two free throws."

I step up to the line, start to go into my foul shot routine. Everyone is lined up, waiting for me to shoot. I bounce the ball, take a few breaths.

But I don't shoot.

Instead, I look at Coach Cash and say, "He didn't foul me."

Coach blinks a few times. "I'm sorry?"

"He didn't foul me. That was a clean block. He didn't touch me."

The rest of the guys start to stir.

"I saw it differently," Coach says.

"You always see it differently when it comes to me," I say. I'm into it now, and it feels good. Like a weight pressing down on my chest has been lifted. "You protect me, Coach, and you're extra nice to me, and start me over players who are better than me. I appreciate everything you've done for me, and you've made me a much better basketball player, but I'm not dumb. I know my dad is helping pay for the team. And that's fine, I can't help that, but I don't want special treatment anymore. My teammates don't like it, and I don't blame them. Alonzo is a better basketball player than me, and he should be starting. And he didn't foul me, so I'm not going to take these foul shots."

And before Coach can say anything, I walk over to Alonzo and hand him the ball. "Go in for me," I tell him. "I'm tired."

Alonzo stares at me for a second. He puts his hand up, and wc high-five.

But he doesn't move. "I go in when the Coach tells me to go in," he whispers.

"Yeah, that makes sense."

Coach blows his whistle. "Alonzo! Get in here!"

Alonzo sprints in, and Coach walks over to me.

"I'll deal with you later," he says.

But I'm pretty sure he won't.

For the rest of practice, I can tell something's different. My teammates look me in the eye. They talk to me more on the court. They don't stop the conversations they're having when I walk up to them. The hand-slaps have a little extra sting to them.

I think I know what it is.

It's respect.

As I'm packing up my stuff after practice, I'm trying to figure out what I'm going to say to my dad, when Carter comes up to me. "That was cool, what you did," he says. "I know the guys appreciated it."

"Should have done it a long time ago," I tell him.

He shakes his head. "Well yeah, maybe, but it's never easy standing up to the man in charge. Takes guts. Even if he is your personal coach."

We laugh, and then a crazy idea hits me. Or maybe, not so crazy. "Hey you want to come over to my house tomorrow? I got a great full court."

Carter looks at me like I have two heads. "Full court? You mean, like, two hoops? Are you serious?"

My ears get red with embarrassment as I suddenly realize that was a stupid thing to say. "Uh, well, you know my dad . . . he played college ball and is pretty wound up about basketball."

"You want me to come over tomorrow? Like, three days before we full-on try to whup each other?"

"Yeah," I tell him. "It's, like, I'm sick of taking all this so seriously."

Carter thinks for a second. "Jeez . . . yeah, I guess sure, that'd be cool."

I see my dad walk in to pick me up. He and Coach Cash have a conversation, with Coach doing most of the talking. Then my dad starts heading my way.

"I'll text you the address," I tell Carter. "Gotta go deal with my dad."

"Yeah, I get that. See you tomorrow."

I go up to my dad before he comes over, because I don't really want Carter or anyone else to hear what he's about to say.

"Hey, Dad. You talk to Coach Cash?"

"I did." But he doesn't look mad. "He said you stood up for a teammate. Good for you." I reach down for my gym bag, but my dad picks it up for me. "Let's go home," he says. "We're having salmon."

I glance over at Coach Cash. He doesn't smile, but he nods. I nod back.

I guess respect is contagious.

I'm sitting in my usual spot at lunch—last table on the right, by myself—when I feel a shadow standing over me.

I look up and see Janeece Renfro.

"You never came and sat with us the other day," she says.

"I didn't think you meant it."

"Callie might not have meant it, but I did."

I take a bite of my sandwich. "Okay. Tomorrow, maybe."

But she doesn't walk away. Instead, she says, "Can I sit here?"

Before I can answer, she sits.

We eat in silence for a few minutes, then she says, "Are you mad at me?"

"I'm not mad at anyone," I tell her.

"Oh."

"I'm mad at everyone."

She stops chewing. "I . . . well, I . . ."

I wait, and when it becomes clear she's stuck, I say, "Are you trying to say that you're sorry, and that you believe me, and that you wish this whole thing never happened?"

Janeece smiles in relief. "Yes."

We keep eating, and after another minute, Carter Haswell walks up.

"Hey," he says.

I give him an extremely fake smile. "Wow, this is seriously my lucky day! The two basketball superstars. To what do I owe the honor?"

He laughs awkwardly. "Can I join you guys?"

I shrug. "If you promise to buy me an ice cream sandwich."

He laughs and sits. "I'll see what I can do."

"Hey I heard you're back on the team," Janeece says to Carter, with a smile that's not at all fake. "Congratulations."

He blushes. "Yeah, thanks."

I look at them looking at each other, and it occurs to me that these two might actually really like each other. And then, for some reason, I realize that if the two of them ever got married, their kids would be seriously incredible basketball players.

But Carter didn't sit with us to flirt with Janeece. He's here to talk to me.

"You know, that day . . . in Ms. V's class . . ."

"You don't have to say anything."

"No, I want to." He swallows, and it occurs to me he might be nervous. Carter Haswell, basketball legend, is nervous talking to me! I make a mental note to remember this moment forever. "When I cheated, I messed up," he says. "I messed up bad. And I felt so guilty, so mad at myself, that when I came back into the room and saw you there—I guess, like, it was easier to pretend all my horrible feelings about myself were just horrible feelings about you. And then today, Ms. V told me that you didn't say anything, and you weren't going to say anything, that actually you were about to leave when I came in to talk to her. And as soon as she said it, I realized, I kind of knew that all along, but I just didn't want to admit it to myself, because if I couldn't stay mad at you, then I would have to be mad at myself. It was really lame, and I'm sorry."

"You know, Carter," I say, "everyone in this school thinks I told on you and got you kicked off the team. I've had to eat lunch by myself for a long time because of you. Did you ever think about that?"

Carter doesn't answer. He just hangs his head.

I watch him, and I realize this could go one of two ways. I could be as immature and unforgiving to him as he had been to me.

Or I could be better than that.

"I'll make you a deal," I tell him. "I'll forgive you if you come on my radio show today."

He lifts his head. "Are you serious?"

"Totally."

He grins. "You got it."

I turn to Janeece. "You have to come on the show, too."

Her eyes twinkle. "With Carter?" she says.

"Yup."

"Let me think about it," she says, even though we all know she doesn't have to think about it one bit.

WWMS
WALTHORNE SOUTH RADIO

ALFIE: Hey everyone, this is Alfie Jenks and
              welcome to Talking Sports. Joining
              me today are basketball superstars
              Janeece Renfro and Carter Haswell.
              It's the last week of the regular
              season, and both the girls and boys
              teams have their traditional season-
              ending games against Walthorne North.
              The girls team is having a great
              year, in first place, while the boys
              team will be fighting it out with
              North for the last playoff spot. But
              the good news is that Carter, who
              has not been with the team for most
              of the season, will be back for this
              final game. Janeece, let's start
              with you. Congratulations on such a
              great year.

JANEECE: Thanks, Alfie. It's really been a dream
              season. All the girls have pulled
              together and it's so fun to go out
              there and compete as a team.

ALFIE: What do you think your secret is?

209

JANEECE: I think we believe in each other and just love the game. I mean, we take it really seriously, don't get me wrong, but we're also loose, we have fun together.

ALFIE: Winning is always fun, right?

JANEECE: That's for sure.

ALFIE: What about you, Carter? How does it feel to be coming back after such a long layoff?

CARTER: It feels great. I'm so excited. But can I . . . can I just say something to your listeners?

ALFIE: Sure.

CARTER: I—I want to apologize to everyone in the school for what I did. I broke the trust of my teacher and everyone around me, and it was a terrible mistake. But, uh, also, I want to apologize to Alfie Jenks. Because she did nothing wrong. She didn't tell on me, or tattletale, or whatever you want to call it.

I thought she did, and I wanted to
believe she did, but I think part of
me knew she didn't, I just wouldn't
admit it to myself. So I just want to
say to everyone, and especially Alfie,
I'm sorry.

JANEECE: Whoa. That was intense. Respect,
             Carter.

CARTER: Don't respect me. Respect Alfie.

ALFIE: Thank you for saying that. It means
             a lot.

CARTER: It's the least I could do.

JANEECE: Carter, are you coming to our game?

CARTER: Uh, um . . .

JANEECE: Are you serious? We're 16–3, dude!
             We're leading the league!

CARTER: I know that, I was just, you know,
             so excited about coming back that
             I haven't thought that much about
             anything else, you know—

JANEECE: It's Thursday night. The night before
              your game.

CARTER: Uh . . . yeah, of course, I'll be
              there. I'll bring all the guys, too.

JANEECE: Sweet!

ALFIE: Okay, great, well, thank you both
              for coming on, and thank you Carter
              for saying what you said. I have
              to go because it's time for Social
              Studies. Be sure to tune in to both
              games on WWMS Radio, they're going to
              be great! This has been Alfie Jenks,
              Talking Sports!

I can tell the second Carter walks in that he's never been in a house like mine before.

"Whoa," he says. "This is like something you see on TV. I didn't think houses like this actually existed in real life."

"Well, yeah, they do."

We go into the kitchen, where my mom is making herself a smoothie. She welcomes Carter with a big smile. "Hello, it's so good to meet you! I've heard you're back on the AAU team, which is wonderful! Why don't you two grab a treat?"

We walk over to the cupboard, which is filled with all sorts of healthy snacks. Carter stares, and I can tell that he has no idea what most of them are. My mom helps him decide. "Here, try one of these power bars. They're healthy but delicious."

Carter smiles. "I didn't know healthy but delicious was a thing."

My mom laughs way too loud. "You're funny! I gotta run to pilates. Austin, be sure to give Carter the full tour. He'll probably get a kick out of the house."

As soon as she's gone, I say to Carter, "You don't really want a tour, do you?"

He gives me a look. "Uh, based on the looks of this place, it might take the rest of the day."

"There are rooms in this house even I've never seen," I tell him. "Let's skip it."

We end up on the basketball court, of course, but we barely play. Instead, we mostly talk.

"So, how long have you been working with Coach Cash?" Carter asks.

He flips me the ball, and I go in for a lazy layup. "Yeah, um . . . kind of as far back as I can remember, I guess."

"Whoa. That's a long time."

"Tell me about it." I realize I've never really talked about this with anyone before. "I mean, the guy is like a total basketball genius and an amazing coach, but it's been like, all basketball all the time, and after a while you start to think, like, is it worth it?"

"Yeah, I get that," Carter says. "You're a really good player, though, for real."

"Ha, thanks. I'm pretty good. I'm not great. Despite my

parents' best efforts. Especially my dad's. If I don't play in college, it's going to break his heart."

"Will it break your heart?"

I laugh. "Absolutely not." It feels good to say that out loud, once and for all.

Carter casually palms the basketball, which is something I can't do. "So why do you keep doing it? I mean, the way you were talking at practice the other day made it sound like you don't even really like playing that much. So what gives?"

I think about that for a few seconds, then say the only answer that seems to make sense. "I don't know. I love basketball. There are just things about it I don't love."

Carter looks around the full court. "I guess your parents are really into hoops though, huh."

I laugh. "Yeah, you could say that. My dad thought he had a shot at the NBA. Didn't happen for him." I cock my head at Carter. "You might have a chance, though."

"Don't say that, man," Carter says. "That's what got me in all that trouble in the first place."

I have a sudden urge to get off the court. "You want to check out my video game set-up?"

"Oh dude, you know it."

We go inside and head toward the rec room, which is downstairs. When I get to the basement door, though, I realize Carter's not behind me. I go back and find him in the living room, staring at the walls.

"What is all this stuff?" he says, his eyes wide.

I shrug. "Art, I guess. My mom is really into it."

Carter starts walking around the room, checking out the paintings, which makes me realize that I've never really looked at them before. They're all really modern, which means they're a bunch of shapes and colors that seem pretty random to me. But I guess they're cool or important or something, because when people come over, my parents always bring them in here to ooh and aah.

Carter stops in front of a sculpture of an eagle. "What's this?"

Amazingly enough, I actually know a bit about this one. "Oh, yeah. We were in Santa Fe a few years ago and my mom saw that in an art gallery. I think it's by some famous artist."

"Santa Fe? Where's that?"

"New Mexico."

The way Carter looks at me, I may as well have said Mars. "Huh," he says. "I've never been out of the state."

He goes to pick up the sculpture, but I stop him. "Whoa, you can't touch it, sorry," I say quickly. "My mom freaks out about stuff like that. Especially with this one, because of what happened."

Carter steps back. "What do you mean?"

"Oh, there was this thing a few months ago where some worker guy dropped it and it chipped." I point at the eagle. "See? It looks like it's got an injured wing. I think it looks kind of cool, but my mom totally lost it. She was so mad, because I guess it's worth a lot of money." I start walking toward the basement door. "Come on, let's go play. Isn't your mom picking you up in, like, twenty minutes?"

But Carter doesn't move. He's just staring at the eagle sculpture. Then he slowly sits down on a couch.

"Dude?" I say. "You good?"

He doesn't look at me. He just stares straight ahead.

"Nah, man. I'm not good. I'm not good at all."

I'm not sure what to do, but I know I can't stay in this house another minute.

I bolt up from the couch and start running toward the front door.

"What is happening, bro?" he asks. "Why are you freaking out?"

I really want to get out of there, but I know he's not going to just let me leave without telling him why, and part of me wants to tell him anyway. So I do. "That 'worker guy' you're talking about is my dad," I say, trying to keep my voice calm. "He's a painter. He paints houses. Or, at least he used to. He lost his job. Because of your mom. And it wasn't his fault. He told her she needed to move the stupid freaking sculpture thing, but she refused. And then after it fell, she goes running to my dad's boss and the guy had to fire my dad. So yeah, I need to go. Now."

But Austin is blocking the door. "That was your dad?"

"Yes. I just said that."

"Dang, bro, I had no idea."

"Well, now you know. He told me the whole story, and I know he was telling the truth, but he said no one would believe him anyway because you guys are so loaded and rich people always get their way and treat other people like crap."

I wait for him to say how bad he feels, to say he's sorry. But that's not what happens. Instead, his face turns angry. "Listen, Carter, I don't know exactly what your dad told you, but he was careless and screwed up. He knocked over the sculpture. I know you want to believe him, but I know what happened. Just because we live in this, like, big house, people want to blame us for everything, but my mom didn't do anything wrong."

We stare at each other, and it feels like all the blood in my body suddenly catches fire. "You don't know what you're talking about. I'm not blaming your mom because you have artwork all over your house and travel to places I've never heard of and your dad bought your way onto the AAU team. I'm blaming your mom because my dad doesn't lie. He told me what happened."

Austin looks stung, like I just slapped him or something, but he doesn't back down either. "My mom doesn't lie either. You can believe what you want to believe."

"So can you."

"AND BESIDES, YOUR DAD WAS DRINKING ON THE JOB!"

It feels like time stops. "What did you just say?"

He stares down at the floor. "Nothing."

My eyes start to fill with tears. There's nothing left to say, really, but that doesn't stop me. "I should have known," I tell Austin. "I should have known this was a dumb idea, coming to your house. We go to different schools. We live in different worlds. Our schools hate each other. We're playing you in two days. This whole idea of being friends was so freakin' dumb."

Austin stands up as straight as he can, which is still about five inches shorter than me. "I agree."

I get out my phone and check the time. "My mom is going to be here soon. I'm going to wait at the end of the driveway."

"Fine."

"Thanks for the power bar." I open the door and walk out. Halfway down the driveway, I hear Austin slam it shut.

WALTHORNESPIRIT.COM

Wednesday at 7:20 pm

Janeece Need to make sure everyone comes out tomorrow night to the game against North . . . last game before playoffs

Like · Reply

Wednesday at 7:24 pm

Sandra I'll be there babe you know it

Like · Reply

Wednesday at 7:31 pm

Antoine What time's the game

Like · Reply

Wednesday at 7:33 pm

Janeece 7

Like · Reply

Wednesday at 7:37 pm

Carter I'll be there and I'm bringing all the boys, we're so ready for this

Like · Reply

Wednesday at 7:42 pm

Sham Everyone wear red

Like · Reply

Wednesday at 7:45 pm

North4Eva What if we don't want to wear read

Like · Reply

Wednesday at 7:48 pm

Briscoe Oh here we go

Like · Reply

Wednesday at 7:52 pm

Kevin We'll see you guys there, it's going to be so much fun, we're going to cheer for our school and show school spirit and just say nice things about everyone. Go team!

Like · Reply

Wednesday at 7:57 pm

Chase Hahahaha I love it

Like · Reply

Wednesday at 8:03 pm

Austin Yeah we'll be there, it will be a good way to warm up for the main event the next night

Like · Reply

Wednesday at 8:05 pm

Janeece Dude are you for real? The MAIN EVENT is OUR GIRLS TEAM which is 16 and 3

Like · Reply

Wednesday at 8:07 pm

Lucas Hahahahah you tell him Janeece
But yeah the next night we will whup up on you all

Like · Reply

Wednesday at 8:08 pm

North4Eva We got Clay coming back people

Like · Reply

Wednesday at 8:11 pm

Sham We got Carter

Like · Reply

Wednesday at 8:15 pm

Kevin We all remember what happened last time, don't we?

Like · Reply

Wednesday at 8:19 pm

Lucas I do, your boy got injured bad

Like · Reply

Wednesday at 8:20 pm

Chase And then your boy cheated, remember that?

Like · Reply

Wednesday at 8:24 pm

Janeece None of that please, just come and cheer for the girls, then y'all can yell at each other as much as you want

Like · Reply

Wednesday at 8:26 pm

Sham Oh you know it

Like · Reply

Wednesday at 8:28 pm

Clay Looking forward to it

Like · Reply

Wednesday at 8:31 pm

Kevin Clay! Glad you're on board bro

Like · Reply

Wednesday at 8:33 pm

Carter Janeece we got you

Like · Reply

Wednesday at 8:34 pm

Sham Ha Carter you wish you got Janeece

Like · Reply

Wednesday at 8:35 pm

Janeece Watch it boys

Like · Reply

Wednesday at 8:36 pm

Austin Janeece I didn't mean anything by it
Looking forward to seeing you play tomorrow
But your boys team is going down the next day

Like · Reply

Wednesday at 8:39 pm

Lucas Ooh big talk I like that

Like · Reply

Wednesday at 8:41 pm

Austin Yeah we're done here

Like · Reply

ALFIE:
Hello everyone and welcome to another great night here at the Walthorne South Gym, my name is Alfie Jenks, sports reporter for WWMS News. The Walthorne South girls basketball team has been on a tear all year, led by the fantastic Janeece Renfro, who is averaging 17 points, 8 rebounds, and 5 assists a game. But they face a very strong opponent in Walthorne North, who despite losing their best player earlier in the season is in third place in the league and riding a four-game winning streak. Both teams take the court in front of a raucous crowd, with big rooting sections from both schools. We're just about set for the tip-off . . .

. . . And midway through the second quarter, Walthorne North takes a time-out, with the score 24–19 in favor of Walthorne South. As expected, the game has been pretty close, but the South girls seem to have things pretty well in control. The same cannot be said

for the crowd, especially the student
sections, as they seem to be getting a
little rowdier as the game goes along.
I did see one teacher go over and talk
to them, so hopefully things will
settle down a bit . . .

AUSTIN

It's only the second girls basketball game I've been to in my life, not including my sister's games. My mom always says that girls play the game the way it's supposed to be played. My dad gets a little mad whenever she says that, but during the first half I understand what my mom is talking about. They cut, they pass, they use the back door, they find the open man—I mean woman—and they zip the ball around. It's not all drive-and-kick-for-a-three, or isolation one-on-one.

I'm impressed.

But my friends are less impressed. We're sitting way up in the bleachers, in the last couple of rows, and the South kids are right across the aisle from us, in the next section over. So of course, everyone starts messing with each other. Eric, Kevin, and Chase kind of start it, making faces and pointing, and their guys do it back. For most of the first half, it's kind of chill like that, kind of funny, although at one point in the second quarter some teacher from South comes over and tells us to settle down.

And everyone does settle down, for a while.

At halftime, a bunch of us decide to walk around the gym to get some food and say hi to some other people. In the aisle, I see Carter, and he sees me. We both look away.

We're halfway down the bleachers when a big guy from South steps in front of us. "Fancy meeting you boys here," he says. "You all ready for the big game tomorrow?"

I feel like I should probably be the one to answer, but before I can, Eric jumps in.

"Oh yeah, you bet we are," he says. "We're more than ready. You ready, chump?"

The big South kid snorts. "Chump? I think you mean champ."

"No, I mean chump." Eric looks around for comic approval, and a few kids laugh, but the rest of us just stand there, ready to get moving.

"Aight, then." The South kid steps aside, and it looks like he's about to let us pass, but then he blocks the aisle again. He's looking right at Eric, but I'm glad to see he's still smiling at least.

"You know, I would appreciate it if you didn't call me a chump. My name is Amir. What's yours?"

"Uh, Eric."

"Nice to meet you, Eric. I look forward to seeing you on the basketball court tomorrow night, where we can get to know each other a little better."

"Okay, yeah," Eric says. "Whatever, sure."

The kid Amir finally steps aside, and we all hurry down the bleachers before anything else happens.

When we're in the hallway outside the gym, Eric takes a deep breath. It's only then that I realize he was nervous.

"Dude," I say. "Are you okay?"

"Yeah, I'm fine," Eric says defensively. "I can handle myself. Which is a good thing, because I didn't see any of you guys jumping in to help me out." He glares at Kevin. "Like, where were you, dude?"

Kevin snorts. "What, you want me to come to your rescue? Not gonna happen."

"What did you want us to do?" I ask Eric. "They're just kids, like us. And besides, you're the one who called him a chump."

"It's cool," Eric mumbles. "Whatever. I gotta use the bathroom."

Kevin, Clay, and I decide to walk over and check out the concession stand. Chase is already there. When he sees us coming, he flashes a fifty-dollar bill. "Hey boys, what's your pleasure?" he says, flapping his money around. "They got a pretty lousy selection of food at this dump, no surprise, but at least they got hot dogs. Anybody want one?"

"Nah, man," Kevin says. "And put that money away." Kevin always thought Chase was a prep-school tool. He's never really liked him. I can see why.

Chase goes to put his bill away, but it's too late—some South kid spotted it. "Yo bro," the kid yells, "mind paying for us?"

Chase grins. "Yeah, uh, I don't think so, but how about we place a little bet on the game tomorrow night, whaddya say?"

"I'd like that," the kid says. "It'll be like taking candy from a baby. How much you wanna bet?"

Kevin tries to step in by saying, "We're not interested," but then Clay chimes in: "How much can you afford? If anything?"

"Nicely played," says some other South kid. "But will we be able to say that after we whup up on you guys by thirty?"

And the next thing you know, kids start lobbing jabs back and forth:

"You're not whupping anyone by thirty, except maybe, let me think . . . oh yeah. Nobody."

"Is nobody your last name?"

"Nobody is my grandma's last name, she's seventy years old, and she's about the only one you can beat on the basketball court."

At some point I hear Carter say, "We'll beat you like a bass drum in a marching band," and I say back, "You're gonna wanna JOIN the marching band after we're done with you."

Chase howls at that one. "Oh, you dropped that one on him good, PJ!"

Carter makes a face. "PJ? Why'd you call him PJ?"

Chase leans toward Carter. "That's his nickname. Short for Private Jet. That how he rolls, yo!"

Carter shakes his head in disgust. "Of course it is."

WWMS
WALTHORNE SOUTH RADIO

ALFIE: A surprising run by North here in the
              third quarter has tightened this game
              right up, and South is only up by one,
              43–42. The fact that Janeece Renfro
              has been in foul trouble has certainly
              not helped. The star guard has only
              been on the floor for fourteen minutes
              so far. There is a definite buzz in the
              air right now. If North found a way to
              pull this game off, it would be quite
              the upset . . .

AUSTIN

I'm still a little wound up from Carter's PJ dig during the third quarter, but I forget about it as the game gets closer. Their best player is in foul trouble and our girls make a run, which of course gets our guys going.

"We're in your ratty old gym and we're still about to beat you!" someone yells in the direction of the South section. Then one of their guys hollers, "This time tomorrow night will be a very different story, my friend! Money can't buy everything, and it DEFINITELY can't buy you a W tomorrow night!"

And just like that, jabs start going back and forth again. It's all pretty harmless until Eric yells, "Hey, Southies! You ever heard the phrase, 'cheaters never prosper'? Look it up!"

Well, that gets people's attention.

Other people in the bleachers start staring at us, and I can feel sweat pop out on my forehead. "Cool it, man," I tell Eric, but the damage is done. I see Carter stand up and make his way toward us.

He steps into the aisle and stares at Eric. "What did you just say?"

Eric turns red, but for some reason he decides to go in even harder. "Come on man, you're a cheater, and your coach got fired because he told you to cheat. Everyone knows it. And even if we lose and don't make the playoffs, we'll still get to go to our beach condos on vacation. If you guys lose, where you gonna go?"

I glare at Eric. "What are you doing, dude?"

Carter gets up in his face. "Oh, is that right? So because you boys get the fine school in the fine part of town, and play in that fancy gym with the fancy scoreboard, you think the rules don't apply to you? It's cool for your pal PJ here to pressure his teammate to play on a bum ankle, or some girl to keep going to school and playing on the basketball team even though she moved to another town? Is that what you're saying?"

I try to calm things down. "Yo, Carter, he didn't mean anything by it."

But Carter isn't in the mood to be calm. "He didn't mean anything by it? Then why'd he say it twice? He didn't mean it twice?"

A few other kids get up, and I see a couple of teachers

heading our way, and I'm not really sure where this is going, but before anything else happens, the third quarter ends, Carter goes back to his section and sits down, and I think that might be the end of it.

It's not.

ALFIE: Well, it all comes down to this,
            folks. After putting the South team
            on her shoulders for much of the
            fourth quarter, Janeece Renfro has
            just fouled out with ninety seconds
            to play and South up by two. It was
            a questionable call, but the way the
            crowd is screaming at the refs is
            completely ridiculous. How are the
            two student sections, who have been
            pretty rowdy all night, supposed to
            behave better when they see adults
            screaming like this? It does make you
            wonder. Walthorne North center Jackie
            Lawlor steps to the foul line—if she
            makes both shots, then we'll have
            a tie game. She bounces the ball,
            takes a deep breath . . . the crowd
            is quiet . . . she makes the first!
            It's a one-point game! Jackie gets
            set for the second shot . . . oh what
            was that? What was that? Someone just
            yelled an obscenity . . . it sounded
            like it came from one of the student
            sections . . . the crowd has suddenly
            erupted again . . . both student

sections are screaming . . . the
refs have stopped the game as several
teachers and administrators rush over
to try and calm things down . . . it
looks like there is some pushing and
shoving going on . . . this could get
ugly, folks . . .

The teachers keep a close eye on us during the fourth quarter, but I still send some glares over at the kid who called me a cheater. He doesn't look at me once. Meanwhile, Janeece is lighting up the place, hitting shots from all over the floor. But the North girls hang tough, and it's going down to the wire.

Then, with, like, a minute to go in the game and South up by two, someone on North drives to the hoop. Janeece steps in front of her, establishes position, and the North girl runs right over her. A total charge. But instead, the ref calls a blocking foul on Janeece. Which means she fouls out of the game, and two shots for the North girl. It might have been the worst call I've ever seen in my life.

And of course, the parents start screaming at the referees.

"THE REFS SUCK!"

"WHAT GAME ARE YOU WATCHING?"

"YOU'RE A DISGRACE!"

And way worse than that, if you can believe it.

Sure enough, the North parents start yelling back at the South parents.

"LEAVE THE REFS ALONE!"

"STOP YELLING, THEY'RE JUST DOING THEIR JOB!"

"*YOU'RE* THE DISGRACE!"

Lucas elbows me in the ribs. "Yo, how come the teachers aren't telling them to settle down, the way they told us to?"

I laugh. "I know, right? I mean, where do they think we get it from?"

Janeece goes to the sideline. She looks like she's about to cry. I have a weird feeling in my stomach, and I wonder to myself, what's that about? Does that mean I really do like this girl? *I should ask her out*, I say to myself, *maybe to a movie. I wonder if she likes movies?*

Then I start laughing at myself. I'm sitting here watching Janeece look so sad on the sidelines, and all I can think about is going on a date with her!

I'm about to ask Sham what's wrong with me when I hear a voice from the North section yell, "THAT'S RIGHT, NUMBER 23, YOU'RE DONE! GO BACK TO WASHING DISHES AT MY COUNTRY CLUB!"

Hold up.

Janeece is number 23.

I shoot up out of my seat, stomp across the aisle and scream, "WHO SAID THAT?" I'm not thinking, I'm just acting. Or more like reacting. "COME ON, WHO'S THE COWARD WHO SAID THAT?"

People behind us are telling me to be quiet, and the North girl is about to take the foul shots to try and tie the game. I'm not sure what to do when Amir suddenly stands up and starts hollering at Austin. "Aren't you the captain of this team? You going to let your team talk trash like that? You going to let your boys disrespect this girl? That's pathetic."

Austin refuses to look at Amir. "I don't know who said it," Austin says. "And whoever it was didn't mean anything. Everyone makes stupid comments sometimes, don't sweat it."

Someone behind us says, "Sit down, you're blocking the view."

I turn to Austin. "Come on, man, who said it?"

"I don't know who said it! Can we just move on? There's, like, a minute left in the game."

I shake my head. "You guys talk smack all game long, but that crossed the line, man. That crossed the line."

Suddenly, someone at the far end of the row stands up and

says, "I said it, okay? I said it. I mean, who fouls out of a close game with a minute left to go? That's pretty dumb."

I point at the guy. "You need to stop talking. Right now."

The guy grins—the grin of a rich kid who thinks he can say and do anything and get away it. "I'll tell you what," he says. "She's a cute girl, so if you think I was so mean, then maybe you can introduce us after the game and I can apologize to her up close and personal."

That's all it takes.

My blood starts to boil, and I decide I'm going to wipe the smirk off that kid's face myself.

I start climbing over the North kids, all of them, stepping on some, ignoring the complaints as they try to push me off, and I get so close to the jerk's face that I'm pretty sure some of my spit gets in his eye.

"SHUT UP! JUST SHUT THE F UP!"

Except I don't say F. I say the whole word.

And I don't exactly say it, I scream it.

And I scream it when the whole rest of the gym is silent, as the player is about to take her second foul shot, to try and tie the game.

AUSTIN

Well, that pretty much does it. After Carter swears at Chase at the top of his lungs, it's like a stick of dynamite whose long fuse has just run out. Everything explodes. Chase jumps up and pushes Carter. Carter pushes him back. A bunch of South guys run across the aisle into our section, and there's more pushing and shoving and yelling. The girls on the court are standing there, not sure what to do. The refs leave the court. Some fans around us start to scatter, while others try to break it up. A bunch of adults are rushing toward us. I want to leave, but I'm trapped in the chaos.

It occurs to me that this could get a lot worse before it gets better.

I see Mr. Rashad and Principal Marshak running up the bleachers, heading straight for us. Alfie Jenks is right behind them. We're still pushing and shoving and yelling, but the guy I was jawing with ducks away and disappears.

"COWARD!" I yell, even though I have no idea where he is.

Mr. Rashad gets to our row and starts yelling, "Enough! Enough!" while Principal Marshak talks into a walkie-talkie. The pile starts moving itself backward, away from Mr. Rashad and Principal Marshak. I'm at the end of the row, and I realize I'm getting pushed closer and closer to the railing that's supposed to protect people from falling off the edge of the bleachers.

That's when I notice Janeece, on the bench, staring up at me with her mouth wide open.

AUSTIN

I can tell that Carter is trying to keep his balance as the crowd starts pushing, away from the adults. The pile is moving him backward, toward the end of the row, but no one seems to notice. I start shoving my way toward him. He's getting closer and closer to the edge, and I'm almost there. Finally, I reach out and try to grab him, but instead I trip and fall into Clay, who is between me and Carter. Clays trips, too, and falls backward, into Carter. It's like a horrible game of dominoes, and Carter is the last domino.

There's no place for him to go.

He starts to stumble backward.

And suddenly, I know exactly what's going to happen before it happens.

CARTER

Seriously?

After all this?

I feel myself lose my balance, and at first I think the railing is going to save me, but then I realize it's too low—I think it's meant to protect people who are sitting down, not people who are standing up and shoving people and screaming swear words.

My back goes over first. I reach out for the railing with my hands but miss.

And then, I feel nothing but air.

I'm falling.

And that's when I realize, when you're falling through the air, about to crash into a hard wooden floor and get really badly hurt or possibly die, you have a lot of time to think.

Which is good, because I have a ton of stuff to think about as I fall.

The first thing I think is, this isn't as scary as I thought. I mean, it's definitely scary, but it's also calm.

And silent.

Like, the world stops.

I keep falling.

I think about everything that happened that led up to this moment.

I think about my mom and dad.

I think about not wanting to die.

I think about how much it's going to hurt when I land, if I don't die.

I think about what kind of injuries I'm going to have and how long it will take for me to get better.

I think about how the injuries might be so bad, I won't be able to play basketball again for a long time. Or ever again.

Or maybe I'll be able to play, but I won't ever be as good as I am right now.

And I think about how that might not be the worst thing in the world.

And then, I run out of time to think.

I hit the floor.

I hear a *SLAM!* Then a *CRACK!*

And everything goes dark.

FRIDAY, MARCH 20 10:27 AM

Final Middle School Basketball Game Canceled

It was announced this morning that the boys basketball game scheduled for tonight between Walthorne South Middle School and Walthorne North Middle School has been canceled.

In a joint press release, the Central Youth Athletic Conference (CYAC) and the Walthorne Board of Education stated, "In light of last night's events at the girls basketball game between the same two schools, we have decided that it is in the best interests of all parties involved to cancel this game. We hope to sort out the various unfortunate issues that have complicated what should have been an annual highlight for these schools, as well as the players and our community. In the near future, we hope to be back cheering for our wonderful student athletes."

The statement is referring to an incident last night in which students from both schools got into an altercation at the end of the girls game that led to one student-athlete falling off the bleachers and getting severely injured.

"It's a real shame," said Walthorne South Principal Valerie Marshak, in a phone interview. "The terrific kids at our school and at W-North work hard for this all year, and now it's been taken away from them. But at this point, I think the decision is the right one. The last thing anyone wants is for tonight's game to be marred by another incident that we all regret. It's only a game, after all."

No one at the CYAC or Board of Education was available for comment.

OVERTIME

CARTER

So yeah, I didn't die, just FYI.

I ended up with a concussion, a chipped bone in my left elbow, torn ligaments in my left ankle, four broken ribs, and a badly sprained lower back.

I should make a full recovery. "For life, and for basketball," the doctor said, "and not necessarily in that order!" Everyone laughed. I tried to laugh, too.

At the hospital, the nurses were all so nice. The food was horrible. I got a lot of cards and flowers and stuffed animals, but I told my parents I didn't want any visitors.

Coach Benny came anyway.

"Hey, kid," he said. "How ya holding up?"

"A little tired, to be honest, Coach," I told him. "But I guess I'm pretty lucky, all things considered."

"I guess that's true." His voice was smaller than usual. "I owe you an apology, son."

"No, you don't. It was my fault. I'm the one who cheated."

"Yes, I do." He sat down in the chair next to the bed. "I look back at what I said to you that day in the cafeteria, and when I think about it honestly, I realize that maybe I did want you to cheat on that test. Maybe I did want to win that badly, and have a great season, and I knew those things couldn't happen without you. I can tell myself I didn't, but I wouldn't be being honest with myself. Or with you."

My back was killing me, and I felt incredibly tired, but I still knew how hard it must have been for him to say that. "I appreciate that, Coach. And thanks a lot for coming by to say so."

He might have said something back to me, but I can't be sure, because I think I was asleep by then.

ALFIE

When I decided to become a sports reporter, I thought it would just be reporting scores and talking about great games and great players and great plays. I had no idea that everything would be so much harder than that. I had no idea that there was a lot about sports that wasn't about what happened on the field or on the court. And that a lot of that stuff was bad.

And then Carter fell and got hurt.

Which is when I decided that something has to change.

Friday at 4:13 pm

Alfie Hey everyone, it's Alfie Jenks. I don't want to bother anyone, especially since we're all still in shock about what happened last night. But I didn't sleep at all, and as I was up thinking about stuff, I remembered this page, and how in the past, everyone would just use it to fool around and make fun of each other and sometimes say stupid or hurtful things. And it seemed harmless at the time but look where that got us. Carter is in the hospital. So I was thinking maybe this time we could change it up and write supportive stuff and actually show some Walthorne Spirit. Sorry to be cheesy but I just think it might help. Let me know what you guys think.

Like · Reply

Friday at 4:15 pm

Sham Thank you for doing this Alfie. I texted Carter a few times and he hasn't hit me back yet, but bro if you're reading this we love you

Like · Reply

Friday at 4:17 pm

Sadie I was at the game last night and it was amazing because you girls on the court were so awesome, but I gotta say I was a little shocked at the crowd, I know our guys didn't act great and the north kids too but the adults were the worst—screaming and complaining and acting like it was a matter of life and death, I mean come on!! #rolemodels
#not
I love you all though, even you North people, Carter, I can't wait to see you back out there soon xx

Like · Reply

Friday at 4:22 pm

Chase Hi my name is Chase Crawford. I just want to apologize to Janeece Renfro for saying that she worked at my country club. Obviously, she's too young to work there. But I'm pretty sure her parents, aunts, and uncles all do.

Like · Reply

Friday at 4:25 pm

Janeece Hi Chase, thank you for saying that, because in case anyone had any doubt, it's now official—you are the biggest jerk in Walthorne. I'm glad you go to private school, and hopefully you'll stay there next year so none of us have to see you at Walthorne High. Oh, and btw what's wrong with working at a country club? As long as it's not YOURS!!

Like · Reply

Friday at 4:26 pm

Chase Yo I'm just kidding around, suddenly everyone needs to be so serious? Look I feel bad that kid got hurt but to be honest he kind of started it

Like · Reply

Friday at 4:27 pm

North4Eva Hey this is Eric and I just want to say that I agree with Janeece, Chase you can be funny but right now you are being a complete jerk, and what you yelled at Janeece was so incredibly gross, it actually made me kind of embarrassed to even know you. Also btw she could completely kick your butt and everyone knows it. And everyone else, I'm sorry for all the trash talking and stuff and also I just want to say to Carter Haswell that I hope he gets better soon because he is literally the best basketball player I've ever seen.

Like · Reply

Friday at 4:31 pm

Lucas Thanks Eric, if there are any other North kids on this thread I want to say sorry for mouthing off at you guys, I mean obviously I didn't know what was going to happen but I said some things that weren't cool and I just want to say sorry about that

Like · Reply

Friday at 4:34 pm

Janeece Alfie, I know you and I talked about this but I just want to say publicly that i feel so bad for what you had to go through for the last few months, it wasn't fair at all, we should have believed you all along and I'm sorry, and I think you're an awesome sports announcer and I can't wait to see you on espn one day

Like · Reply

Friday at 4:35 pm

Alfie Thank you Janeece and that would be so awesome. I have a long way to go, but I'm just really happy about what people are writing here

Like · Reply

Friday at 4:37 pm

Kevin This is cool, glad you're doing this, I play for North and man I'm really embarrassed about last night, and to Alfie, thanks for doing this and we shouldn't have given you a hard time on this page a few months ago, that was bogus, sorry bout that. also just fyi my parents grounded me for two months, so I'll see everyone NEVER.

Like · Reply

Friday at 4:40 pm

Sham Hahahahaha that's hilarious, I mean not the Alfie part, the grounding part of course lol

Like · Reply

Friday at 4:42 pm

Kevin It's cool I deserve it

Like · Reply

Friday at 4:45 pm

Sham Anyone else get grounded?

Like · Reply

Friday at 4:47 pm

Janeece Not me ☺

Like · Reply

Friday at 4:51 pm

Eddy My parents told me we were gonna sit down tonight and talk about it and when I asked what does that mean they said "you'll see" 😕

Like · Reply

Friday at 4:52 pm

Amir You're done dude

Like · Reply

Friday at 4:53 pm

Eddy Oh I know it

Like · Reply

Friday at 5:02 pm

Clay If anyone knows how Carter is doing please let me know, also what hospital is he in coz I'd like to send him a card or something, I don't know him but I hear he's a good dude

Like · Reply

Friday at 5:05 pm

Janeece He is a good dude

I'll find out the hospital

Like · Reply

Friday at 5:08 pm

Austin Hi Alfie, I don't know you but thank you for doing this. Sorry I'm a little late to the party but I've been reading these posts so far and they're really cool. First off, I want to apologize to Janeece for not dealing with Chase at the game, after that disgusting thing he said to you . . . that was pathetic of me and I'm really sorry. And secondly, yeah I can confirm that Carter Haswell is a good guy. A lot of you probably don't know this but I remember Carter from a long time ago, we used to play basketball in the park. I was taller than him back then and almost as good lol. Anyway we're also on the AAU team together so I've gotten to know him again and he came over to my house earlier in the week and we hung out. I guess my point is that rivalries are fun but making them personal is stupid, and everyone says and does things they don't mean and wish they could take back. I hope everyone is doing okay and Carter if you're reading this I hope you're doing okay and I'm sorry about the other day at my house too

Like · Reply

Friday at 5:11pm

Janeece What happened the other day?

Like · Reply

Friday at 5:12 pm

Austin I was totally uncool that's what happened

Like · Reply

Friday at 5:14 pm

Alfie Austin thanks for what you said and I'm really bummed I'm not going to be able to call the game tonight, you guys have a really good team

Like · Reply

Friday at 5:17 pm

Austin Thank you

Like · Reply

Friday at 5:19 pm

Lucas I totally remember free shoot! Hey Clay I was really looking forward to that rematch dude, I'm glad your leg is better

Like · Reply

Friday at 5:21 pm

Clay Thanks man, appreciate it

Like · Reply

Friday at 5:22pm

Lucas Next year on freshman team, teammates?

Like · Reply

Friday at 5:23 pm

Clay For sure, unless I make varsity lol

Like · Reply

Friday at 5:25 pm

Sham Oh you're playing varsity, you and Carter for sure

Like · Reply

Friday at 5:26 pm

Clay We'll see but thanks
#teammates

Like · Reply

Friday at 5:27 pm

Lucas #teammates

Like · Reply

Friday at 5:28 pm

Kevin #teammates

Like · Reply

Friday at 5:30 pm

Sham #teammates

Like · Reply

Friday at 5:31 pm

Janeece #teammates

Like · Reply

AUSTIN

Over the next week, it turns into a bit of a thing.

People go on Walthornespirit.com every night. More and more kids join, just saying hey, comparing schools, talking about nothing, getting to know each other. I realize that even though we're in the same town, our school and their school are incredibly different. We have new tennis courts with new nets. They have old basketball courts with no nets. It doesn't seem fair. No wait—it's NOT fair. Next year, a lot of us are going to be in high school together, so we might as well start figuring out what we all have in common.

But there's one person who hasn't joined the party.

I texted Carter five times the day after it happened, but he never responded. A few days later, his friend Lucas posted about all of Carter's injuries. As bad as it sounded, it could have been so much worse. Lucas said Carter hasn't been back to school since it happened.

I try texting a bunch of times over the next few days.

No answer.

So I decide to do something shocking.

I decide to not rely on my phone.

CARTER

The pain is bad, but the boredom is worse.

It's been ten days, and it still hurts to move. A big day for me is going from the bed to the couch. I've watched pretty much every episode of every bad reality show there is.

I know every SportsCenter announcer's first name, last name, and middle initial, because I stare at them all day long.

For the first week, I played a lot of guitar, but then I broke a string and my mom hasn't had time to get it fixed.

The other day I even read a book that wasn't assigned in school!

Okay, fine, I *started* a book.

But as bored as I've been, the one thing I haven't been interested in is seeing other people, or even talking to them. I just don't feel like it. Besides, I know exactly what they would say.

I can't believe that happened.

I'm so glad you're going to be okay!

How are you feeling?

Are you bored?

When can you play basketball again?

So I'm lying here, trying to do my math homework (as if things aren't bad enough), when there's a knock on the door.

My mom's at work, so she can't answer it.

My dad doesn't live here, so he can't answer it.

You can probably guess by now that I don't really feel like answering it.

So I just shout, "WHO'S THERE?"

It takes a few seconds, but then I hear, "It's Austin. Austin Chambers."

"Who?" I ask, even though I heard it pretty clearly.

"Austin Chambers."

"Oh. Um, can you come back later? I can't really get to the door right now."

"Uh, sure, no problem. You weren't answering my texts so I thought I'd come by. Hope you're doing okay."

"Yeah, I'm okay, thanks man."

"Okay, take care."

I hear his footsteps drift away, and I lie back and close my eyes, relieved that that's one less thing I have to deal with.

My relief lasts two minutes.

Because then the door opens, and my dad walks in with a brown paper bag in his hand. Austin is right behind him.

"Hey ho!" my dad says. "I found this fellow just leaving. He says he was here to see you." My dad doesn't come close enough for me to tell if there's alcohol on his breath. I choose to think there isn't.

"Dad, this is Austin Chambers. I told you about him, remember?"

My dad's face slowly changes as he remembers the name. "Oh, yeah, of course." He looks at Austin. "How are things, son?"

"They're okay, sir," Austin says.

"No need to call me sir."

"Got it." Austin shuffles his feet, like, he's nervous. "Uh, Mr. Haswell, I want you to know that I know about what happened at my house a few months back, and I'm really sorry about that. I'm sure it was a misunderstanding, and I don't think my mom had any idea you lost your job over it."

"Oh, I think she might have had some idea," my dad says. "Anyway, I'm feeling a little better about the whole thing these days, because a few days ago your mom made a call to my boss Rico, and she said she may have gotten the circumstances of the incident wrong, after all. He's agreed to bring me back on, starting next week."

"Dad!" I try and sit up for a second, and that's all it takes for my back to tell me to lie the heck back down. "That's great news!"

"Well, Cartman, it's a whole lot better than a sharp stick in the eye." My dad puts the paper bag down on the table. "Anyhoo, I just came by to bring you lunch. Bologna sandwiches, my personal fave." He starts walking toward the door.

"You're not going to stay?" I ask him.

He shakes his head. "Nah. I got stuff to do. New paintbrushes to buy." He nods at Austin. "Plus, you got company. I bet you two have plenty of ground to cover."

I bet we do, too, but that doesn't mean I want to cover it.

After my dad leaves, Austin picks up the bag. "Want a sandwich?"

"Sure, thanks."

There's another one there, but he doesn't take it.

"Help yourself," I say.

He hesitates. "I'm not really allowed to eat that stuff."

"What stuff?"

"Processed food."

"Says who?"

"My parents."

"They're not here."

Austin thinks about that for a second, then picks up the sandwich and takes a bite. "Whoa, that's good," he mumbles, with his mouth full.

"Bologna is the best."

We eat silently for a minute or so, then he says, "I can leave if you want."

"Nah, it's cool."

"Okay." He looks around and says, "Do you mind if I get some water?"

"Of course not," I say. "The glasses are above the sink."

"Cool, thanks."

Austin gets up and walks into the kitchen. I can see him looking around, checking things out, peeking his head into the living room. He hesitates.

"Something wrong?" I ask him.

"Nah, I'm good," he says, but he's just standing there.

"What's up?"

"Can I tell you something, honestly?"

"Yeah."

He gets the water, then comes back and sits down. "I've . . . I've never been in an apartment before."

"Are you serious?"

"Yeah, I'm serious. Like, how many rooms do you guys have here?"

"Four. My bedroom, my mom's bedroom, the living room, and the kitchen. And the bathroom, so I guess five."

"Huh," Austin says, but I can tell by his face what he's probably thinking: *We have five bathrooms, and they have five rooms total.*

I don't really want to talk about the differences between my apartment and his mansion, so I change the subject. "How's AAU going?"

"Oh, it's going okay. We have another sleepaway tournament next weekend."

"That should be fun."

"I guess. We were all a little out of it at the last practice. Coach Cash was getting really mad. I think everyone is a little freaked out about your injury."

"Join the club."

Austin laughs, then shifts uncomfortably. "So, are you . . . like, did the doctors say when you could play again?"

"They're hoping three months," I tell him. "But they say I'll be as good as new. I guess I got really lucky."

"Wow, okay." Austin glances at my back brace, my arm in a sling, my ribs all wrapped up, and I'm guessing he's thinking that I don't look that lucky. But I am.

"I got your texts," I tell him. "I'm sorry I didn't text back."

"No, it's cool. I just wanted to see how you were doing."

"Well, I really appreciate that you came by."

"Of course. That's what friends are for."

I feel this weird feeling come over me. Like I'm about to cry. I decide to blame the medicine.

"So, does this mean, like, we're friends again?" I ask.

"I think so." Austin half-smiles. "I hope so."

Neither of us says anything for a few seconds, then he adds, "When you came to my house, I . . . uh . . . I'm really sorry about what I said about your dad."

"Thanks," I say. I haven't done much talking in the last week—none, basically—and all of a sudden it feels like I need to make up for lost time. "When you reminded me that we used to play ball together back in the park, I remembered you as being such a nice kid. And then you were cool at AAU, too. And I thought to myself, yeah, we could be friends. But then when I went over to your house, I mean . . . I was like, how can I be friends with someone who lives in a house like this, you know? How is that even possible?"

"That shouldn't have anything to do with it," Austin says.

"But it does," I say. "I mean, my dad was, like, a handyman at your house. Just some worker. And your mom thought he did something wrong, and who knows, maybe he did do something wrong and maybe not, but that's a fight he's never going to win, right?"

"It's not about that," Austin says. "People who are different can be friends, if they have other stuff in common. Like, I mean, we've both spent our whole lives playing basketball, right? And we both have mixed feelings about it." He leans back in his chair, and he looks like he's starting to relax for the first time since he came into the apartment. "Like, my dad was a basketball star in college, right? And I was supposed to be tall and a great player like him. I trained hard, spent hours analyzing just about every game I ever played. I even had a special diet, and I could only have ice cream if we won. But it didn't work. I wasn't a great player, and I was never going to be a great player. And when I saw you play that first game of the year, I thought, that's what I'm supposed to be. And it made me mad, you know? But then, when Clay came back, we played a game of one-on-one, and he beat me, and the world didn't end. And that day at AAU practice when you came back, and I didn't take those foul shots, and my teammates started treating me with respect, everything just kind of changed for me. I realized I could let the dream go. I could still love basketball, but it didn't have to be everything to me anymore. Winning didn't have to be everything. I didn't have to tell a kid to play hurt. I didn't have to be the leading scorer or the best player. I didn't have to care that much. I just didn't."

Austin stops talking and looks at me. Waiting for me to respond. So I do.

"It's been a little different for me, I guess."

"What do you mean?"

I hesitate, at first. Then I start talking.

"You wanted to be better than you were, but I kind of wanted to be worse than I was." It's not something I've ever said out loud, or even realized before. "Everyone thinks it must be totally awesome to be so good at something, and sometimes it is. Sometimes it's the greatest feeling in the world. But sometimes it's not. Sometimes it's too much. Too much attention, too much pressure, too many expectations. I mean, look what happened with the cheating thing—I don't even love basketball that much, but even so, I did, like, this really dumb thing, because I thought I had to. I literally thought it was the only choice, that if I couldn't play basketball then everything would be ruined. I mean, I like basketball, I really do. Maybe I even love it. But sometimes it felt like I had to LIVE it. And I didn't want that."

"I did want to live it," Austin says.

"Is that why you cheated too?" I ask him.

Austin looks shocked. "Cheated? What do you mean? I didn't cheat."

"You sort of did, though." He stares at me blankly, and I realize he has no idea what I'm talking about. "Playing on the AAU team because your dad sponsored the team? Taking a spot from some kid out there who's a better player, but who didn't have the money to pay?"

"That's different," Austin says, defensively.

"Kind of different," I say, "but kind of the same."

"You didn't have the money to pay, and you're on the team."

"That's because your dad and Coach Cash knew I'd help them win and build their program. That's how it works, we both know that."

Austin doesn't answer that one, which is fine by me. The last thing I want to do is get into another fight with him. I don't have the strength for it, for one thing. Luckily, he seems to feel the same way.

"I guess things don't always work out the way we want them to," I say, finally.

"Or maybe they work out exactly how they're supposed to."

My phone buzzes, and I look down. It's my mom, texting that she's working an hour late, but bringing fried chicken home for dinner.

BOOO, I text her back, BUT ALSO YAY!!!

"How about now?" Austin asks. "How do you feel about basketball now?"

"When I come back," I tell him, "I'm gonna start over. And maybe learn to love the game, you know, on my terms."

"That sounds about right."

We fall silent. We're both breathing kind of hard, like all that talking took something out of us. I shift the pillows under my head. My elbow starts to hurt. It's like my injuries are in some kind of pain rotation, and now it's my elbow's turn. Later, my back will want a turn, I know that much.

"I should go," Austin says.

"Okay," I say.

"Can I come visit again?"

"Yeah, that'd be cool."

"Awesome."

I shake my head. "Man, everything was so much more chill when it was just a bunch of us playing in the park, wasn't it?"

"Oh, you know it," Austin says, laughing. "Free Shoot. Running around, sweating, playing game after game until they told us we couldn't play anymore."

"Just pure ball. That's what I want. That's what I miss."

I close my eyes to remember. I can almost hear our little kid voices, and feel the hot black concrete under my feet, and taste the lemonade I used to buy from the hot dog guy.

I open my eyes.

"Hey, I got a crazy idea," I say. "I mean, it's nothing we can do right now, but when I'm better, it might be kind of cool."

Austin looks curious. "What is it?"

I tell him.

Turns out he doesn't think it's so crazy, after all.

DOUBLE OVERTIME
Three Months Later

ALFIE: Hello everyone, and welcome to
           another exciting day of basketball.
           Even though the official season ended
           a while ago, we have one last game
           to bring to you today. But I'm not
           coming to you from the Walthorne
           South Gymnasium, where I usually call
           games. No siree, today we're here at
           the beautiful Tompkins Park courts,
           where the Panthers of Walthorne South
           will be taking on the Cougars of
           Walthorne North. That's right, the
           boys basketball game that was canceled
           way back in March has been rescheduled
           for today. Not by the schools, not by
           the athletic conference, but by the
           kids. They are just going to go out
           there and play. No refs, no audience,
           no adults of any kind. Because that's
           how they want it . . .

AUSTIN

In the car on the way to the park, my dad is talking about how he used to drop me here every Saturday. "Man, we couldn't keep you away from this place," he says. "Kind of like how now, I can't keep you away from your phone."

"Ha ha," I say, my head buried in my phone.

Neither of us mentions the fact that I haven't played much basketball in the last few months, ever since I decided to leave the AAU team. When I told my parents my decision, they were really upset for about a week. They didn't think I meant it. They thought I was just doing it because I was mad at them for getting Carter's dad fired.

But then after a while, they realized something.

They realized I was happier.

And slowly, they accepted it.

My dad pulls the car into the parking lot. "Are you just hanging out with friends? Playing a pickup game? What's this about?" The curiosity over why I grabbed a basketball and asked for a ride to the park is just killing him.

But I'm not about to give it away. "Just felt like shooting around," I say.

"Okay. Well, I gotta work later, so Mom is going to pick you up."

"Cool, thanks for the ride."

"Have fun," he says.

As I walk down the hill to the courts, I realize that I've never heard my dad say those two words to me in relation to basketball before.

I see Carter, and I walk over. "Hey."

"Hey." He looks around. "Man, I haven't been here in a long time."

"We had some great games here back in the day, remember?"

"Yeah, we mixed it up pretty good."

I stick out my hand. "Good luck."

"Same."

We shake.

I gather up the team.

"Hey everyone," I announce, "Amir is going to be captain today."

Amir blinks. "For real?"

"For real. You deserve it."

I start to walk away with the other guys, but Amir puts his hand on my shoulder. "Yeah, yo, uh, Carter?"

I wait for him to say more, but he doesn't, so I say, "What's up? You good with being captain today?"

"Yeah totally." He bends down and starts double-lacing his sneakers. "Anyway, uh, I just wanted to say it's good to see you back on the floor."

"Don't I know it. Thanks, bro."

"You know," he says, "you got a gift."

"A gift?"

"Yeah, man, the way you play this game . . . you just . . . you know, you got the thing."

"Thanks dude, I appreciate that," I say. "You want to, like, form a layup line or something?"

Amir finishes his lacing, straightens up, and looks me right in the eye. "I know you got mixed feelings about basketball, and I get that, honestly, I do . . . but man, it could be your ticket out."

I laugh. "Yeah, my mom's been saying that forever."

"I know she has, and I know it's a ton of pressure, but you gotta realize, a lot of people would kill for that opportunity. A lot of people, myself included. And when you fell, man, that opportunity could have been taken away from you. But it wasn't. You got another chance. Another chance, man."

He pauses, but I don't move. For some reason, I know he's not quite done.

"Don't waste it, is all I'm saying."

I nod. "I won't, man," I tell him. "I promise I won't." And I mean it.

We smack hands, and go out to warm up.

AUSTIN

Everyone's here except Clay. I start to think maybe he's not coming.

"I don't know, PJ," Kevin says. "Maybe he just didn't want to deal with it."

I shake my head. "Nah." But actually, I'm thinking the same thing. I check my phone. No messages.

We start warming up on one end of the court, doing layup drills, dribbling drills, outside shots. I look down at the other end of the court. Carter's guys look really strong.

I start taking a few free throws when Eric points up the hill. "Look!"

Clay is walking toward us. He's got his basketball stuff on. Now he's running.

And he looks ready to go.

ALFIE: There's not a cloud in the sky, and it's a beautiful day for outdoor basketball. And, well, to be perfectly honest, I'm actually not calling this game live. I'm shooting video on my cellphone, which I will edit into a YouTube video for later. Mr. Rashad told me the best broadcasters get their starts by doing stuff like this, so that's what I'm going to do! The players are taking the court, and we're just about set to begin . . .

AUSTIN

After we warm up for a while, I go to center court and yell over to Carter, "Should we do captains?" By that I mean meeting, shaking hands, talking a little bit about the rules. Usually the refs organize all that, but we don't have any refs today.

Carter nods, but doesn't walk toward me. Instead, another kid comes up—tall and serious-looking. I recognize him from the girls game disaster. We shake hands.

"Are you . . . are you the captain?" I ask him. "What about Carter?"

"Carter named me captain today," the kid says.

"Oh, cool," I say, even though I'm confused. "Well, uh . . . I'm Austin."

"I'm Amir."

I realize it's cool that Carter named him captain, and then I get mad at myself for not thinking to do the same thing for Clay.

"Great," I say. "Well, I guess we should talk about a few rules."

"Sure. One time-out for each team per half?"

"Yeah cool. Sub whenever you want?"

"Yeah cool. Two thirty-minute halves, running time, cool?"

"Yeah cool."

Amir tugs at his shirt. I realize he's a little nervous. Then I realize I'm a little nervous.

"Okay," I say. "Well, uh, have a good game."

"You too."

We shake hands again and go back to our own halves of the court. I circle up the guys. "Clay, take the tip. Kevin, Charlie, Eric, Toph, you guys start."

They stare at me.

"You're not starting?" Clay asks.

"Nope. Bring it in."

Everyone puts their hands in a big pile. I put mine in last.

"Let's have fun, on three."

The guys all grin.

"One, two, three, LET'S HAVE FUN!"

ALFIE: Amir Watkins wins the tip, and we're
underway! Carter Haswell gathers the
ball in the backcourt, crosses into the
frontcourt, zips a pass over to Lucas
Burdeen, who goes up for the shot, no
good, Sham Collins gets the offensive
rebound, stripped by Clay Elkind from
North, who passes to another guy from
North—fans, I apologize for not knowing
the names of some of these players, I
don't have rosters in front of me . . .

. . . We're midway through the first
half ladies and gentlemen, and may
I just say that I'm very glad to be
watching basketball the way it's
supposed to be played—hard, fair, and
fun. I can tell you that the game is
pretty even, but I don't know the
score, because there's no scoreboard.
Ooh! Amir just blocked a shot by
someone on North, and the ball goes
flying, but he definitely got some of
the kid's arm as well. Amir is saying
something to the kid . . . I believe
he just called a foul on himself. The
North player goes to the line for two
foul shots . . .

AUSTIN

I go into the game after about ten minutes. The score is 12–8, them. Jerrod and Jake come in with me, Charlie, Eric, and Topher come out, Kevin and Clay stay in. It's our best lineup. South makes a couple of changes, too, but Carter stays in. We match up against each other. He takes the ball upcourt and I hand-check him, just like Coach Cash taught me. He makes a move between his legs and then crosses over in one fluid motion. I stumble a little bit but recover. He dumps the ball into a big guy who just checked into the game. I go over to help out, but the guy spins the ball over his shoulder back to Carter, who is cutting baseline. I'd taken my eyes off him for one second and it cost me. Carter makes the easy layup. I'm mad at myself but I know it was a great play, so I do something that surprises Carter. Something I would definitely never do in a league game. I hold my hand up in front of Carter. It takes him a second to realize what I'm doing. And then he gets it.

We high-five.

CARTER

Austin posts me up. I think he's going to the hoop, but instead he goes up for a midrange turnaround. I try to block it, but I get about two inches off the ground. I'm tired and my legs are rubbery, but there's no way Amir is going to tell me to come out. So I yell over, "Sham, grab me! Need a blow!" Sham's eyes go wide. He's not the best player. Coach Benny never would have pulled me for him. But I don't care. I mean, it's just a game, right? A game I really want to win, don't get me wrong, but still, just a game.

Sham runs onto the court and starts trash-talking right away. It's the best part of his game, because he can really run his mouth. Usually the refs tell him to can it, but there are no refs today, so he's going off.

He lights into this one kid on North, rattling off one dis after another.

"Man, is that all you got?"

"My grandma got more hops than you, and she's in a wheelchair."

"What kind of shot is that, son—you trying to kill the backboard?"

The kid doesn't exactly react the way Sham wants him to, though. He's not getting mad. More like the opposite—he's howling with laughter at everything Sham says. So Sham ends up being the one who gets mad.

And p.s., he doesn't exactly have the greatest hops in the world either.

I ask someone how much time is left, and what the score is. Three minutes left in the half, and it's 22–19, us.

I'm thinking about putting myself back in. Coach Benny would have, for sure. But I decide not to. The clock winds down, under two minutes. Austin goes up for a three and hits it. Took him a while to get going, but it looks like he's got his stroke working. 22 all. Ten seconds left. Lucas tries a last-second shot from the corner but it goes in and out.

Halftime.

ALFIE: Well, that halftime pizza was
                certainly a nice surprise! Apparently
                it was donated by Austin Chambers'
                family, and it was a big hit with
                the players, who are normally not
                advised to eat pizza at halftime of
                a basketball game. I was able to ask
                Austin about it, and apparently he
                called his mom just before the game
                started and asked her if he could
                order pizza to be delivered to the
                park. He assumed she would try to talk
                him into having power bars or celery
                sticks, but instead she said sure,
                why not? He was shocked. And so was
                everyone else when the pizza showed
                up! Now, we're just about set for an
                exciting second half, although we have
                to see if the players show any ill
                effects from gorging themselves on
                cheese and dough . . .

For the last five minutes of the game, we both have our best lineups in. Austin drops two treys in a row. I dish to Eddy for an easy bucket. On the defensive end, Lucas blocks a shot, but Clay grabs the loose ball and spins one in off the glass.

"TIED AT FORTY-EIGHT!" a kid yells. "ONE MINUTE LEFT!"

Suddenly things feel a little tense—no more high fives with the opponents, that's for sure. We bring it down, I have an open three but pass up the shot, flip the ball inside to Eddy, he misses a gimme. The rebound gets knocked around by Amir and Kevin, and eventually the ball goes out of bounds.

Kevin goes, "Our ball."

Amir shakes his head. "Nah, man, off your leg."

"I didn't touch it," says Kevin.

"I saw it, dude," insists Amir. "Definitely caught you behind the knee."

Austin goes over. "Hold up guys, it's all good."

But it's not all good. As the rest of us gather around, Amir and Kevin keep arguing about whose ball it is, and then Kevin says something like "Fine, whatever," and he grabs the ball and throws it down the court.

"What was that, man?" Amir says, raising his voice. Kids are starting to body up to each other, getting a little intense, and my heart starts racing. After a great game, it can't end like this.

"Everyone, let's all just chill!" I yell.

"Seriously!" adds Austin.

No one seems sure what to do. There's no pushing and shoving going on, but kids are getting in each others' faces and I don't like how it feels. Austin looks at me like, *Dude, now what?* And I look back at him like, *Dude, I have no idea.* I stare up into the sky, hoping there's an idea in the clouds somewhere.

And there is.

"HOLD UP! HOLD UP!" I yell. "I GOT IT! I KNOW WHAT WE'RE GONNA DO!"

Everyone stops jabbering and looks at me.

"What?" asks Amir.

I grin. "We're gonna settle this old school."

AUSTIN

We all stand there, waiting for Carter to tell us his great idea.

"Austin," he says. "I need you to help me settle this once and for all."

I look at him cockeyed. "How?"

"Well, our guy says the ball was off your guy, and your guy says the ball was off our guy. There's only one way to find out who's right."

"Which is what?"

He sticks out his hand. "Rock paper scissors."

"Rock paper scissors?"

"Rock paper scissors."

Now I get it. "Just like Free Shoot," I say.

He grins. "Just like Free Shoot."

I look around. Kids are nodding, and it seems like everyone is thinking the same thing.

Why not?

"Okay," I say. "How many takes it?"

"One takes it, just like always."

"Great."

Clay steps up. "I'll say 'rock, paper, scissors, shoot,' and you guys put your hands out on shoot."

Carter and I both nod.

The tension builds.

Here we go.

"Okay, let's do this!" Clay pronounces. "ROCK, PAPER, SCISSORS, SHOOT!"

Carter puts out scissors. I put out paper.

He wins.

"YES!" Carter hollers.

"NOOOOOOO!" I moan.

But to be honest, I'm not mad. Actually, I think it's kind of funny.

I look at Carter. He looks at me. And the next thing you know, we both start cracking up.

The guys on Carter's team go nuts and start pounding him on the back. Meanwhile, I collapse to the ground, pretending to be devastated. My teammates look at me, shaking their heads and smiling. Eventually I get up, walk over to Carter, and shake his hand. "You won fair and square," I tell him. "Scissors beats paper every time. Dang, I need to practice more."

Everyone laughs.

It's almost like we forget that we have a game to finish.

ALFIE: Well, the game has just ended, ladies
                and gentlemen, and I don't think I've
                ever seen anything quite like that.
                A very intense contest comes down
                to the last few seconds, one final
                disputed possession, and the argument
                is settled by rock paper scissors. You
                won't see that in an official league
                game, that's for sure. During the
                postgame handshakes, the kids on both
                teams were laughing and high-fiving
                each other, which is another thing
                I've never seen in all my years—well,
                two years—of covering boys basketball.

                    Oh, by the way, Walthorne South
                ended up beating Walthorne North by
                two, on a last-second shot by Sham
                Collins. Everyone thought Carter
                Haswell was going to take the shot,
                but after he was triple-teamed he
                found Sham for a wide-open layup.
                Congratulations to the South kids, but
                really, congratulations to both teams
                for reminding us all how the game is
                supposed to be played.

                    Thanks for tuning in! This is Alfie
                Jenks reporting.

AUSTIN

After the game, kids start to drift away, biking home or getting a ride from their parents. When my mom comes to pick me up, Carter walks up to her.

"Hi, Ms. Chambers."

Her face looks unsure. "Nice to see you, Carter. How are you?"

"I'm fine. Austin played really well today."

"Was it fun?"

"It sure was."

"I'm so glad to hear it." My mom looks at me. "Dad will be glad to hear it, too."

"I promise to tell him all about it later," I say. She looks a little skeptical, but I mean it.

Carter shifts his feet. "Ms. Chambers, I heard you called my dad's boss and helped him get his job back. I'm not sure what happened that day at your house, and I know it's complicated, but I just wanted to say thank you."

"You're very welcome," my mom says. "My son really respects you. I hope you know that."

"I do," I say, looking at Austin. "And I respect him, too."

My mom looks around. "Are your parents coming to pick you up?"

"Nah," Carter says. "I'm just going to walk."

"Are you sure?" my mom asks. "Don't you live a couple of miles from here?"

"It's fine. I like walking."

An idea occurs to me. "Hey, Mom? I'm going to go with Carter."

Now my mom looks really surprised. I'm not big on walking long distances. "Wait a second," she says. "Who are you and what have you done with my son?"

I laugh. "Well, at least part of the way."

My mom throws up her hands, but she's smiling. "Call me if you need me. Good to see you, Carter."

"Good to see you, too," he says.

After my mom leaves, I look around and realize we're the only ones left. And I'm still holding the basketball.

"Hey, can I get a rematch?" I ask Carter.

He laughs, but then realizes I'm serious. "Now?"

"Yeah, now. We beat you guys first game of the season, you beat us today. Rubber game, you against me, for all the marbles."

Carter grabs the ball out of my hands and starts spinning it on his finger. "Okay, why not? Let's do it."

Neither of us says the obvious thing, which is that he's way better than me and it's probably not going to be much of a game. But hey, you never know, right?

We shoot it out to see who gets the ball first. Rock, paper, scissors.

He goes rock.

I go paper.

"You got me this time," he says, tossing the ball back to me. "Let's do this."

Game on.

We're playing to twenty-one, twos count as twos, threes count as threes, loser takes the ball out, gotta win by two.

We don't talk much. We just ball.

The game is tight, because even though I've got the height and the moves, he keeps dropping threes on me. Plus, I'm not gonna lie, I'm not in the greatest shape after my layoff, and my legs are real heavy.

He's up 20–19 when I drop in a baseline jumper. 21–20, me. Austin takes the ball out, starts to dribble. His handle is decent but I'm quicker, and I flick the ball away—all I have to do is grab it and go in for the layup, and this thing's over. But the ball bounces off my shin and right back into his hands. I'm off-balance, which gives him the split second he needs. He spots up at the three-point line and lets it fly. It looks good leaving his hands. We watch the ball. It might go in and it might not. But either way, we both know two things.

One: At that moment, there's no place we'd rather be.

And two: No matter who wins, we're gonna go get ice cream.

AUTHOR'S NOTE

Hi everyone, thanks for reading my book!

You may or may not have noticed that this is the second story I've written that takes place in the fictional town of Walthorne. The first, *Game Changer*, was inspired by my son Jack's middle school and high school football career. For *Rivals*, I've moved on to my son Joe, who has always loved basketball, and who had a dad (me) who was willing to drive him all up and down the East Coast to various tournaments. Watching Joe playing basketball, like watching Jack playing football, provided me with a close-up look at all that is wonderful and worrying about kids and sports.

For Joe, the games were great, and the friendships that he forged will hopefully last a lifetime. But after a while it became clear that his basketball life was not just about playing games and making friends. It was about taking something that's supposed to be fun and turning it into a job. And that's what our youth sports culture has become. The pressure to win, to succeed, to be special, to use athletics to get ahead, has become more important than just going out there and running around, having a blast, and getting some exercise in the process. And the money it takes to succeed in this pressure-cooked environment—for specialized coaching, for elite teams, for travel—puts a particular burden on many lower-income children and families.

Whenever I do school visits, one of the first things I tell the kids is that there are two sides to every great story. And there are definitely two sides to *this* story. Teaching our kids to compete is great, but teaching them a win-at-all-cost attitude is not; the desire to excel is to be encouraged, but the immense pressure to be the best is not; giving our children the means to succeed is noble, but the uneven playing field caused by the massive cost involved is not.

A few years ago, I read about an initiative called "Don't Retire, Kid." Launched by The Aspen Institute's Project Play in partnership with ESPN, the project was designed to convince the youth of America not to give up—and give up on—sports. Its message is simple: *Remember when sports were fun? Let's make them fun again.* I think that's a message worth sharing, which I've tried to do here.

I hope you enjoyed the book—now go out there and play!

Your pal,
Tommy G

For more information, I recommend visiting the following sites and articles:

www.aspenprojectplay.org/dont-retire-kid
www.aspenprojectplay.org/youth-sports-facts/challenges
www.nytimes.com/2019/09/22/us/school-football-poverty.html
www.browndailyherald.com/2019/09/03/aman-20-time-make-
    youth-sports-fun
www.theatlantic.com/education/archive/2017/09/whats-lost-
    when-only-rich-kids-play-sports/541317

ACKNOWLEDGMENTS

Let's see how many sports clichés I can cram into one acknowledgments section:

Thank you to the brilliant Erica Finkel, who always comes through in the clutch. Erica, I'm not sure how much you know about sports, but you certainly know a tremendous amount about editing sports-themed books.

To everyone at Abrams, especially Emily Daluga, Jenny Choy, Brooke Shearehouse, Trish McNamara O'Neill, Melanie Chang, Megan Carlson, Jenn Jimenez, Marcie Lawrence, and Andrew Smith, you guys always knock it out of the park. I'm so grateful to be a part of your winning team.

Brianne Johnson and Allie Levick, the very definition of cool under pressure—thank you for bringing your A game every time out.

Thanks to my kids, Charlie, Joe, and Jack, and my niece Jessica and nephew Jake, for your excellent notes. The five of you constantly answered the bell, always stepped up to the plate, and never dropped the ball. Because of you, writing this book was a total layup.

And finally, to my wife, Cathy—you're in a league of your own.